Praise for the Night Stalkers series:

"Top 10 Romance of 2012."
– Booklist, *The Night Is Mine*

"Top 5 Romance of 2012."
–NPR, *I Own the Dawn*

"Suzanne Brockmann fans will love this."
–Booklist, *Wait Until Dark*

"Best 5 Romance of 2013."
–Barnes & Noble, *Take Over at Midnight*

"Nominee for Reviewer's Choice Award
for Best Romantic Suspense of 2014."
–RT Book Reviews, *Light Up the Night*

The Night Stalkers

Christmas at Steel Beach

The Night Stalkers

Christmas at Steel Beach

by

M. L. Buchman

Buchman Bookworks

Other works by this author:

Romances

-The Night Stalkers-
The Night Is Mine
I Own the Dawn
Daniel's Christmas
Wait Until Dark
Frank's Independence Day
Peter's Christmas
Take Over at Midnight
The Night Stalkers Special Features
Light Up the Night
Chistmas at Steel Beach

-Firehawks-
Pure Heat
Wildfire at Dawn
Full Blaze

-Angelo's Hearth-
Where Dreams Are Born
Where Dreams Reside
Maria's Christmas Table
Where Dreams Unfold
Where Dreams Are Written

Thrillers

Swap Out!
One Chef!
Two Chef!

SF/F

Nara
Monk's Maze

-Dieties Anonymous-
Cookbook from Hell: Reheated
Saviors 101: the first book of the Reluctant Messiah

Dedication

To the USS *Peleliu* and those who built and served on her.
Many thanks for your thirty-seven years of service.

Note:
The USS *Peleliu* was launched in 1978 and is due to retire in 2015. The ship and the LCAC's are as accurate to real-life as I could make them. To those who served on her and know better, my apologies.

Chapter 1

U.S. *Navy Chief Steward* Gail Miller held on for dear life as the small boat raced across the warm seas off West Africa.

The six Marines driving the high-speed small unit riverine boat appeared to think that scaring the daylights out of her was a good sport. It was like a Zodiac rubber dinghy's big brother. It was a dozen meters long with large machine guns mounted fore and aft. The massive twin diesels sent it jumping off every wave, even though the rollers in the Gulf of Guinea were less than a meter high today.

Gail wondered if they were making the ride extra rough just for her or were they always like this; she suspected the latter. Still she wanted to shout at them like Bones from *Star Trek*: *I'm a chef, not a soldier, dammit*. But being a good girl from South Carolina, she instead kept her mouth shut and stared at her fast-approaching new billet.

The USS *Peleliu* was an LHA, a Landing Helicopter Assault ship. She could deliver an entire Marine Expeditionary Unit with her helicopters and amphibious craft. Twenty-five hundred

Navy and Marines personnel aboard and it would be her job to feed them. All the nerves she'd been feeling for the last five days about her new posting had finally subsided, buried beneath the tidal wave of wondering if she was going to survive to even reach the *Peleliu*.

At first, the ship started out as black blot on the ocean, silhouetted by the setting sun that was turning the sky from a golden orange over to more of a dark rose color.

Then the ship got bigger.

And bigger.

In a dozen years in the Navy she'd been aboard an aircraft carrier only once, and it lay twenty minutes behind her. She'd been there less than a half hour from when the E-2 Hawkeye had trapped on the deck. They'd shipped her to the *Peleliu* so fast she wanted to check herself and see if she was radioactive.

It didn't matter though; she was almost there. From down in the little riverine speed boat, her new ship looked huge. The second largest ships in the whole Navy, after the aircraft carriers, were the helicopter carriers.

Gail knew that the *Peleliu* was the last of her class, all of her sister ships already replaced by newer and better vessels, but even six months or a year aboard before her decommissioning would be a fantastic opportunity for a Chief Steward. Maybe that's why they'd assigned Gail to this ship, someone to fill in before the decommissioning.

Fine with her. She was still unsure how she'd actually landed the assignment. She'd spent a half-dozen years working on the Perry Class frigates as a CS, a culinary specialist. Her first Chief Steward billet had been at SUBASE Bangor in Washington state feeding submariners while ashore until she thought she'd go mad. She missed the ship's galleys and the life aboard.

Then she'd applied for a transfer, never in her life expecting to land Chief Steward on an LHA. After the aircraft carriers, they were the premier of Navy messes. Chefs vied for years to get these slots and she'd somehow walked into this one.

No, girl! You've cooked Navy food like a demon for over a decade to earn this posting. Her brain's strong insistence that she'd earned this did little to convince her.

And she hadn't walked into this, she'd flown. It had taken three days: Seattle, New York, London, Madrid, and Dakar, each with at least six hours on the ground, but never enough to get a room and sleep. And then an eyeblink on the aircraft carrier.

It didn't matter. It was hers now for whatever reason and she couldn't wait.

The LHA really did look like an aircraft carrier. She knew it was shorter and narrower, but from down here on the waves, it loomed and towered. *One heck of an impressive place to land, girl.* She could feel the "new posting" nerves fighting back against the "near death" nerves of her method of transit over the waves.

The flattop upper deck didn't overhang as much as an aircraft carrier, but that was the only obvious difference. Like a carrier, the Flight Deck was ruled over by a multi-story communications tower superstructure and its gaggle of antennas above.

On the deck she could see at least a half-dozen helicopters and people working on them, probably putting them away for the end of the day. It seemed odd to Gail that they were operating so far from the carrier group. It had taken an hour even at the riverine's high speed to reach the *Peleliu* and she appeared to be out here alone; not another ship in sight.

In the fading sunset, the ship's lights were showing more and more as long rows of bright pinpricks. The flattop was at least five stories above the water.

The riverine boat circled past the bow and rocketed toward the stern. Gail had departed the aircraft carrier down a ladder on the outside of the hull amidships. But here they approached the stern.

That was the big difference with the LHAs; they had a massive Well Deck right inside the rear of the ship. She'd seen pictures, but when her orders came, they'd been for "Immediate departure." No time to read up on the *Peleliu.* So, she'd learn on the job.

A massive stern ramp was being lowered down even as they circled the boat. It was as if the entire cliff-like stern of the boat was opening like a giant mailbox, the door hinging down to make a steel beach in the water.

Also like a mailbox, it revealed a massive cavern inside. Fifteen meters wide, nearly as tall, and a football field deep; it penetrated into the ship at sea level. Landing craft could be driven right inside the ship's belly, loaded with vehicles from the internal garages or Marines from the barracks, and then floated back out.

The last of the fast equatorial sunset was fading from the sky as the riverine whipped around the stern at full-speed in a turn she was half sure would toss her overboard into the darkness, and roared up to the steel beach.

Inside the cavern of the Well Deck, dim red lights suggested shapes and activities she couldn't quite make out.

# # #

The sunset was still flooding the Well Deck through the gap above the *Peleliu's* unopened stern ramp as U.S. Navy Chief Petty Officer Sly Stowell did his best to look calm. After nineteen years in, it was his job to radiate steadiness to his customers, the troops he was transporting. That wasn't a problem.

He was also supposed to actually *be* calm during mission preparations, but it never seemed to work that way. A thousand hours of drill still never prepared him for the adrenaline rush of a live op and tonight he'd been given the "go for operation." This section of the attack—presently loading up on his LCAC hovercraft deep inside the belly of the USS *Peleliu*—was all his.

"Get a Navy move-on, boys," he shouted to the Ranger platoon loading up, "'nuff of this lazy-ass Army lollygag."

A couple of the newbies flinched, but all the old hands just grinned at him and kept pluggin' along. They all wore camo gear and armored vests. Their packs were only large for this mission, not massive. It was supposed to be an in and out, but it was always better to be prepared.

Two of the old hands wore Santa hats, had their Kevlar brain buckets with the clipped on night-vision gear dangling off their rifles. It was December first and he liked the spirit of it, celebrating the season, though he managed not to smile at them. It was the sworn duty of every soldier to look down on every other, especially for the Navy to look down on everyone else. It was only what the ground pounders and sky jockeys deserved, after all.

The *Peleliu* was a Navy ship, even if she'd switched over from carrying Marines to now having a load of Army aboard. The transition had worried him at first. Two decades of Marines and their ways had been uprooted six months ago and now a mere platoon of U.S. Army 75th Rangers had taken their place. The swagger was much the same though.

But *Peleliu* had also taken on a company from the Army's Special Operations Aviation Regiment—their secret helicopter corps. They didn't swagger, they flew. And, as much as Sly might feel disloyal to his branch of the Service, they tended to bring much more interesting operations than the Marines.

He could hear the low roar as the engines on the Ranger vehicles selected for this mission were started up in the *Peleliu's* garage decks. The three vehicles rolled down the ramp toward Sly's hovercraft moments later.

Normally it would have taken an hour of shuffling vehicles to extricate the ones they wanted from their tight parking spaces. But fifty Rangers needed far fewer vehicles than seventeen hundred Marines. The whole ship now had an excess of space. Having a tenth of the military personnel aboard had meant that two-thirds of the Navy personnel had also moved on to other billets.

Sly had been thrilled when his application to stay had been granted. It might not be the best career move, but the *Peleliu* was his and he wanted to ride her until the day she died.

It had also turned out to be a far more interesting choice, though he hadn't known it at the time. Marines were all about *invade that country,* or *provide disaster relief for that flood or earthquake.* The 160th SOAR and the U.S. Rangers were about fast and quiet ops that only rarely were released to the news.

He watched as his crew began guiding the M-ATVs onto his hovercraft. They looked like Humvees on steroids. They were taller, had v-shaped hulls for resistance against road mines, and looked far meaner.

He'd been assigned to the LCAC hovercraft since his first day aboard. First as mechanic, then loadmaster, navigator, and finally pilot. And he'd never gotten over how much she looked like a hundred-ton shoebox without the lid.

Sly kept an eye on Nika and Jerome as they guided the first M-ATV down the internal ramp of the *Peleliu* and up the front-gate ramp of the LCAC. He trusted them completely, but he was the craftmaster and it was ultimately his job to make sure it was right.

The "shoebox" presently had her two narrow ends folded down.

The tall sides were made up of the four Vericor engines, fans, blowers, defensive armor, and the control and gunnery positions. The front end was folded down revealing the three-lane wide parking area of the LCAC's deck. Between the two massive rear fans to the stern—which still reminded him of the fanboats from his family's one trip down to the Florida Everglades where they had not seen an alligator—a one-lane wide rear ramp was folded down toward the stern.

The LCAC was the size of a basketball court, though her sides towered twice as high as the basket. She filled the wood-planked Well Deck from side to side and could carry an Abrams M1A1 Main Battle Tank from here right up onto the beach. Those days were gone, though. Now it was the noise of Army Rangers and their M-ATVs filling the cavernous space in which even a sneeze echoed painfully.

Still, the old girl could handle them and it had instilled a new life in the ship. She'd been Sly's home for the entire two decades of his Naval career and he didn't look forward to giving her up. He sometimes felt as if they both were hanging on out of sheer stubbornness. Hell of a thought for a guy still in his thirties. Hanging on by his fingernails? Sad.

He'd considered getting a life. Mustering out, having a pension in place and starting a new career. But he loved this one.

And he'd been aboard the eight-hundred foot ship long enough that she was now called a two-hundred and fifty meter ship instead. This was his home.

Eighteen year-old Seaman Stowell had nearly shit his uniform the day he'd reported aboard. She'd been patrolling off Mogadishu, Somalia then. In the two decades since, they'd circled the globe in both directions, though since the arrival of SOAR most of their operations had been around Africa. In nineteen years he'd traded East Africa for West Africa…and a lifetime between.

As he did before every mission, he willed this mission to please go better than the disastrous Operation Gothic Serpent— the failure immortalized by the movie *Black Hawk Down* that had unfolded ashore within days of his arrival aboard.

Sly didn't feel all that different, except he no longer wanted to shit his pants before battle. He still had to consciously calm down though.

Instead of a humdrum routine settling in after the Marines Expeditionary Unit's departure, the Rangers and SOAR had amped it back up.

SOAR was a kick-ass team, even by Navy standards. That they also had the number one Delta Force operator on the planet permanently embedded with them only meant that Sly's life was never dull.

That was one of the reasons that Sly was looking forward to this operation. When Colonel Michael Gibson was involved, you knew it was going to be a hell-raiser.

They had the first M-ATV in place and locked down. The second one rolled up the ramp. Lieutenant Barstowe, the Rangers' commander, came up beside him with his Santa hat still in place.

"Chief."

"Lieutenant."

"That's one battle-rigged and two ambulance M-ATVs. Why don't I like that ratio?"

"Because you're a smart man, Chief Stowell." The lieutenant moved up the ramp to talk with the driver of the third vehicle still waiting its turn.

They were definitely going into it heavy. That's what finally calmed Sly's nerves. It was the preparation he hated, once on the move he no longer had spare time to worry that he'd forgotten something.

At least he wasn't the only one sweating it. Today was pretty typical December off the West African coast, ninety degrees and ninety percent humidity. Even the seawater from the Gulf of Guinea was limp with tepid heat as it sloshed against the outside of the hull with a flat slap and echo inside that resounded inside the Well Deck.

The last of the vehicles rolled up onto the LCAC hovercraft. For the Landing Craft, Air Cushion hovercraft—technically pronounced L.C.A.C. but more commonly El-Cack! like you were about to throw up—forty tons of vehicles and fifty Rangers was about a half load. But still he was going to keep an eagle eye on them. These young bucks might think they were the bad-asses, but until they'd faced down a Naval Chief Petty Officer—well, that was never going to happen as long as he was in the Navy.

Nika and Jerome guided the last of the vehicles into position at the center of gravity. Nika had been on his boat for two tours now and she'd better re-up next month because he had no idea who he'd ever find to replace her. She worked quickly on chaining down the third vehicle and then gave him a thumbs up. Jerome had six months as his mechanic, but had the routine down and echoed Nika's signal. His engineer and his navigator reported ready.

The crew had already preflighted the craft, but he liked to do a final walk-around himself. There was only a foot between either side of the LCAC and the Well Deck walls.

The wooden decking along the bottom of the Well Deck was just clear of the wash of the ocean waves, so he didn't need waders to do the inspection. For conventional landing craft that needed water to move around in, they could ballast down the stern, which lowered the ship to flood the Well Deck a meter deep or more. However, his hovercraft didn't need such concessions. It was better this way. They could lift off dry without shedding a world of salt spray in all directions.

"Nika," he called as he headed down to start his inspection, "get that stern gate open." During the loading, the last of the sunset had disappeared, near darkness filled in the gap above the big door.

The Well Deck's lights flickered as they were switched over from white to red for nighttime operations. They hadn't flickered when he first came aboard, but she was feeling her age. He patted the inside of the *Peleliu's* hull in sympathy as he reached the wooden planking that supported his LCAC. The huge rear gate let out a groan and began tipping out and down toward the sea.

His hovercraft was ninety feet long and fifty wide and there actually wasn't much to see during his inspection, which was a good thing. The deflated skirts that would trap the air from the four gas turbine engines, delivering over twenty-thousand horsepower of lift and driving force, now hung in limp folds of thick black rubber. Patches covering tears and bullet holes from prior missions dotted the rippling surface. Above the rubber skirt, the aluminum sides were battered from the hard use—partly bad-guy assholes with rifles and partly harsh weather operations.

Sly saw the former as badges of courage for the old craft... and did his best not to recall how the latter was earned when nasty cross seas had slammed his craft into the sides of the Well

Deck entrance. He was a damn good pilot, but there were limits to what a man could do when the ship went one way, the seas another, and his hovercraft a third.

He was halfway around his craft when he first heard it, the high whine of an incoming boat. It hadn't been there a moment before. The Well Deck acted like a giant acoustical horn, gathering all sounds from dead astern and amplifying and focusing them like a gunshot at anyone inside the cavernous Well Deck at the time. Often you'd hear a boat before you saw it, especially at night.

He stood at the foot of the rear ramp of the hovercraft and turned, but there were no lights to see.

Then there were, incredibly close aboard. A small unit riverine craft by the arrangement of the blinding white lights that had him raising an arm to save his eyes.

The riverine was carving a high speed turn as if they intended to run right up the stern gate and into the Well Deck.

They cut their speed at the last moment with a hard reverse of the engines, but he knew it was too late for him.

The bow wave rushed up the Well Deck planking ahead of the riverine, driven bigger and faster by the abrupt nose-down of the decelerating craft. The wave came high enough to soak him to mid-calf and made him sit down abruptly. The wave washed part way up the rear ramp of his hovercraft before receding—totally soaking his butt.

He wondered who he could blame for this one.

In a moment, he was going to stand up and the fifty Rangers standing on the LCAC's loading deck were going to be laughing their asses off at the Navy's expense.

That just wasn't right.

Sly glared over at the small riverine craft, squinting against the bright array of lights so that he could see who to blame. The bow section folded forward and allowed a tall woman wearing a duffle over one shoulder and carrying a small black case to dismount. Then the craft began backing away from the Well

Deck even as the bow section was pulled back up. He didn't get a good look at any of them. *The dogs!*

The woman walked up close to Sly and stopped to look down at him.

That initial impression of tall was combined with Navy fit, and a uniform that showed it off in the best way. Her short tousle of dark red hair hung perfectly as if she'd just brushed it rather than gone for a ride on a craft that could hit thirty-five knots. She wore an emblem of a large crescent-shaped "C" over four horizontal stripes. The "C" marked her as a Steward, the four stripes as the new Chief Steward they'd been told to expect.

She looked like a breath of fresh air.

Truth be told, she looked like the goddamn goddess Venus rising from the water as she stepped out onto the last retreating sheen of seawater that was washing back off the deck under her boots.

He stood to greet her properly.

A roll of laughter sounded behind him and Sly turned— remembering a moment too late as he turned his back on the new Chief—the butt of his uniform was still sopping wet.

# # #

Chief Steward Gail Miller didn't bother trying to stifle her laugh. It just blew out of her. Her laugh was the main reason of many that her insignia wasn't gold colored with twelve years of "Good Conduct," unlike the Chief Petty Officer with the wet behind.

Somehow, the simple fact that she had laughed in the face of a grumpy ship's Captain three years earlier—after her ship took a bad pitch and roll and she'd dumped a plate of turkey with cranberry sauce she'd been serving him down the front of his dress whites—hadn't worked out so well.

She hadn't done it on purpose.

At least mostly not.

But he was enough of a stiff-necked, stuck-up— Well, when the opportunity presented itself, she hadn't fought too hard to retain her balance. Might have succeeded if she'd tried, might not, but even in retrospect she'd still say it was worth it. However, Gail would make certain she was less obvious next time; she would have been in lockup if saner heads had not prevailed.

Not even yet technically aboard the *Peleliu*, she decided she'd better behave now. She sent the wet Chief Petty Officer a sharp salute as his injured dignity appeared to call for it.

She also noticed that the Rangers had stopped their laughter the very moment he turned to glare at them. The man clearly commanded respect among them—at least under normal conditions.

Gail struggled to suppress the rest of her laugh, but she could feel a broad smile giving her away.

"Permission to come aboard, Chief." You didn't "sir" an enlisted man no matter how high he'd risen or you'd get the standard line about how he "worked for a living."

A look of deep chagrin slid onto his face, and his salute came back with a smile that pulled up on the left side of this lips first. A good smile. A damn good one, proving he wasn't nearly as old-school as he looked at first glance. The initial impression of grizzled old sea-dog was actually a handsome and fit man in his late thirties wrapped up in old-Navy respectability.

"Permission granted, Chief." His voice was deep and friendly despite his recent humiliation. He looked her in the eyes, not the chest, unlike the Marines who had just delivered her from the carrier. His hair wasn't crew-cut short, but rather long enough to make her want to mess it up.

Who knew they even made men like that anymore.

"Sorry about that, Chief," she dropped her salute. "But you gotta watch where you sit."

"Thanks. Helpful." He looked down at his watch. "Welcome aboard. We're out of here in thirty seconds, you better hurry across," he pointed up the ramp and through the crowd aboard the LCAC.

He started up the ramp himself, his boots squishing with each step.

She surveyed the load on the hovercraft. Rangers aboard with combat gear and a trio of M-ATVs looking huge and brutal with a bristle of sharp weaponry. Even the ambulances had turret guns. They were loaded for some kind of exercise. Two Santa hats that stood out among the crowd of Rangers said it would be an easy one. Maybe just transport to do some on-shore relief work.

"Mind if I come along?"

The Chief halted halfway up the ramp of his craft. She was still down on the wood deck. A seaman worked his way through the Rangers and came down to her, clearly there to guide her to the ship's commanding officer to report in.

"Headed into a live op, Chief Steward," the Chief Petty Officer fended her off. He emphasized the last word making it clear where he thought she belonged—in the kitchen.

To him she wanted to say, *I'm a soldier too, not just a chef, dammit.* Granted she only had Basic Training and a yearly one-week refresher, but she was a soldier. Still, it wasn't her style, so she gave him a different answer.

"Excellent!" An actual mission? She'd never been on more than a training sortie. She remembered that as an exhilarating time. How dangerous could this one be when there were Santa hats aboard.

She handed her gear to the seaman, except for her helmet and armored vest, and waved him off to go do what he had to do with her stuff. With the ease of long practice, he disappeared up the ramp and through the crowd of Rangers headed back into the ship.

Gail had just come from one of the most boring galley messes on the planet. SUBASE Bangor had been tedious at best. Submarine crews returned to the shore of Hood Canal and immediately evaporated. The only ones she fed day in and day out were the maintenance and refit workers. She was so glad to be back out on the ships that she didn't dare give the Chief a moment to think.

There might be seven thousand culinary specialists in the Navy, but there were only three hundred Navy messes. If she was ready to command one of those, she was ready to go on an actual mission.

She strode up the hovercraft's stern ramp, but didn't stop beside the nameless Chief Petty Officer still riveted in place halfway up—just in case he came to his senses. Instead Gail continued onto the LCAC's deck, donning her gear as she went. She'd never been on one and was eager to look around anyway.

Three-meter steel walls all around. No, three-meter high walls of machinery. This was a hovercraft, big engines and big fans lined either side of the deck. Glassed-in control station high up forward to starboard. Small observer and gunner station port-side forward. Small steering fans to each side forward.

The monster fans at the tail, each twice her height, were positioned to push the boat ahead.

When she reached the first of the Rangers, she turned back to look at him standing there as if paralyzed. She made a show of checking her watch then looking back at him over her shoulder.

"Ten more seconds, Chief. Aren't we outta here yet?"

She offered him her best smile as the nearby Rangers laughed once more at his complete discomfiture.

Gail was sorry to do it to the man, but it was all in good fun.

# # #

There was a part of Sly Stowell that wanted to drive the woman off his boat, but he had the feeling that was a conversation that wouldn't go quickly and he was out of time. Besides, he had a sneaking suspicion that he'd lose.

A part of him thought that losing to her might not be such a bad thing. His eyes were finally recovering enough from the riverine's glaring lights to inspect her by the Well Deck red night-ops lighting.

She was a nicely built craft, trim in all the right places and generous in the others. There—

She arched one of those fine eyebrows at him and his attention snapped back to reality. He'd been admiring things that a decent man didn't admire on a new Chief, even if she was a Steward and not a Petty Officer.

And if he didn't get on some hustle, he was going to be late to the party.

Fine.

"You," he aimed a finger at her, "are not leaving my side. If you end up dead before you've officially reported in, I'm just gonna roll your body over the side, because I sure as hell don't need the damned paperwork."

Then he looked for Lieutenant Clint Barstowe, suited up just like the rest of his Ranger grunts. Found him right in the thick of it by his red Santa hat—made it easy to respect the man. Leading from the front and keeping the guys at ease. These were all seasoned troops and didn't need their hands held, but it was still well done.

They exchanged nods; no need to speak. *Good to go.*

Sly went.

He turned his back on the new Chief and climbed the ladder up to the control room. Troops weren't supposed to ride out on the Service Deck, out in the open, if at all possible. Half crowded into the small deck houses to either side, the rest squeezed aboard their vehicles.

Even so, no one, except the gunners perched high atop their machines, had a view of anything other than sky. Add in the wild motion of the hovercraft over the Atlantic and he just thanked his lucky stars that he wasn't the one who had to barf out his guts without breaking stride as he ran out onto some hostile beach.

The control room sat atop the right front corner of the hovercraft, a glassed-in room that looked like a miniature airport control tower from the outside and a three-seat passenger jet cockpit from the inside. His engines threw the same force as a fully-loaded 737 in flight and took a lot more skill to fly. No such thing as smooth air in a hovercraft.

Dave and Tom were already in position at engines and navigation.

"Wow! What a great little Christmas tree!" The new Chief came up behind him as he moved into the right-hand seat.

The woman walks into one of the coolest cockpits in the Navy, and remarks on a foot-tall tall Christmas tree.

Well, that told him more about the woman than he'd wanted to know. Why were so many of the really pretty ones brain dead?

Dave had made the little wire sculpture out of green wire and strung it with red-white-and-blue LED lights and a couple strands of red and green plastic beads that were actually a necklace his four-year old niece had sent him. It was cute, but that was about all.

"You!" he pointed at the observer's jump seat. "There!" Why he was being so damned gruff about it was beyond him, but he couldn't seem to get that "new recruit" tone out of his voice. Some part of him must figure it was the only thing she'd understand.

She planted her butt. Thankfully, she'd pulled on her armored vest making her at least somewhat less distracting. She really did have a fine shape. That was one nice thing he liked about having more women in the service over the years, it had definitely served to make a ship's crew more pleasant to look at. Regrettably, unlike most, that appeared to be about all this woman was gonna offer.

"Seatbelt too. You're going to be needing it."

That got her attention and the quick response showed the woman had some sense; she buckled up. He still wasn't sure quite how she'd come to be aboard and didn't have time to unravel it. "Dazzled" was not a state that ever happened to him, but he suspected that it just had.

He moved into the right-hand seat and nodded for Tom to lift the front gate. He had the comms and nav up, so Sly gave Dave the "go" for engine start.

Now things were going to start happening fast.

Like a jet, Dave finished the prestart checklist, and goosed the four gas turbines to life one by one. It was completely deafening as the engines' roar reverberated throughout the *Peleliu's* Well Deck. Even the soundproofing on the LCAC's control room couldn't muffle it. He dragged on his helmet and booted up the displays projected inside his helmet's visor.

When Sly gave him the nod, Dave inflated the rubber skirt that would make it so that they didn't sink like a stone—actually like a giant steel box with no lid—if they experienced a lift failure.

Then Sly fed the power from Dave's engines into the big blowers beneath the deck and spray erupted on all sides. He set the lift control to force the air downward. That blasted the water—that had flowed under the planking after washing his goddamn butt for him, it was still wet and clinging against his seat—up into a blinding cloud of spray which showered back down on the LCAC. He hit the wipers on the three forward windows and the two to the side. Despite that, their view of the Well Deck disappeared in the swirl of self-generated fog.

Nika—a testament to just how good a woman *could be* serving in a Navy uniform—sat in a small turret on the port-side forward corner of the LCAC. He glanced across and saw that her wipers were going as well. Once they were out in the open, she'd call out if he was about to run over anything with her corner—at least anything that he didn't want to. An LCAC was sometimes even better than a tank at nudging things out of the way, like people. Give them a blast of jet-lift air and a taste of heavy rubber skirt and they cleared out plenty fast.

Jerome was down making sure the Rangers and their vehicles were all okay despite the walls of mist now soaking everything and everyone who wasn't hunkered down.

"Craftmaster has the boat," he called out over the radio to his crew. He liked the title. It was as if he became even more than being a Chief in the Navy when he was flying the LCAC, as if such a thing was possible.

He eased back on the yoke for a bit of reverse thrust and backed the boat out away from the steel ramp inside the *Peleliu*. The air driving out to either side kept him centered in the Well Deck. The ship was steaming straight upwind, but the swells were running three-to-five feet. The U.S. Navy was a strange mash-up of metric, standard, and nautical units that never seemed to straighten themselves out.

He slipped down the steel beach of the rear gate of the *Peleliu* and struck clear air over the water. Now all of the generated spray blew out to the sides. However, he still couldn't see a thing.

Pitch dark had hit about an hour ago, and except for the muted lighting of the open Well Deck which revealed the wave height and little more, only the ship's running lights made her visible at all.

He kicked the nose sideways with a twist of the yoke and pushed it forward.

His baby roared to life and leapt away into the darkness.

Chapter 2

*G*ail *was overwhelmed by* the assault on her senses. She'd pulled on her helmet after buckling into the observer's seat. She'd only secured the belt because she did feel bad for the Chief—he squished as he sat down.

As soon as they were clear of the *Peleliu,* the Chief spun the boat—she didn't even know his name yet—and they shot off across the waves. Her helmet slapped back against the rear window with a hard whack that echoed down her spine.

The high whine of gas turbine engines pierced through her Kevlar like it wasn't there and the bass roar of the big fans that lifted and drove the hovercraft pounded against her diaphragm like an awesome Maroon 5 concert from right down in the pit.

By the time she thought to look back, the towering carrier was dwindling from sight. She scrabbled around until she found the comm system cable by her chair and jacked it into her helmet.

"Okay if I ask a question?"

"As long as I don't have to answer."

She wished she could see his face; his tone was so dry, it was hard to read. Humor or macho jerk? Jury was still out. She'd have bet on the latter, except for that great smile he'd lasered at her on first arrival.

The hovercraft rocked and jostled proving that the seatbelt hadn't been some idle suggestion and the padding that she'd thought luxurious at first...wasn't. No way the Rangers down in the deck cabins were having a good time of this.

"How fast can this beast go?"

"Seventy knots if I don't have an Abrams aboard, but the boys down below wouldn't appreciate it in these conditions, so I'm keeping it under fifty."

No wonder the *Peleliu* had disappeared behind; she had no idea these hovercraft were so fast. She hoped that she wasn't upsetting her new commander. Jumping aboard the LCAC had been a whim, and since she was technically not due aboard until tomorrow morning, maybe it would be okay. Besides, a training exercise never hurt anyone; good to know as much as you could about a new berth. She just hoped the master of the *Peleliu* saw it that way and wasn't some Navy hard-core steeped in propriety.

"What are you doing with 75th Rangers? I thought that landing helicopter assault ships were always loaded with jarhead Marines."

"She doesn't know," the guy at the engines station looked over at the Chief driving the boat. "I'm Dave, this is Tom, by the way." The man at the engine console hooked a thumb at his buddy at the nav station, who did that part-way turn thing to acknowledge her presence without fully turning from his instruments to look back at her.

Neither one thought to introduce the Chief, which was getting a little peculiar. But she wasn't going to be the first to ask. Of course, now she had to give her name...or not.

"Hi, guys. What don't I know?"

"What do you think, Chief? Can we trust her?"

The boat jarred over a particularly rough wave but the Chief kept her rock steady; well, steady wasn't the right word, but it was clear he was highly skilled at something that looked wholly impossible. The hovercraft must weigh close to a hundred tons and it shuffled and slewed over the water like a puck on an air hockey table. A barely controlled one. He was constantly making adjustments using foot pedals and a wheel that moved like an aircraft's: side-to-side and in-and-out.

"She's the new Chief Steward," that dry tone again, "maybe we should wait to find out if she can cook first."

"Piss her off, boss, and we just might be eating slop for the rest of the tour."

"Nah," she was catching their rhythm, "just him. Wouldn't do that to y'all."

It got her the easy laugh.

She wasn't going to be doing that to any of them. Her goal was to make this the best damn mess in the fleet. She figured she only had a month or so before the next round of inspections would occur for the Captain Ney Memorial Award for best Navy mess. The "Large Afloat" category filled the gap between destroyers and the enormous aircraft carriers, and she planned to rule it.

Well, they weren't telling her what it was that she didn't know. Maybe they'd lost track of the question, though she'd bet the taciturn Chief hadn't.

Fine, different tack.

"So, what's today's exercise?"

"Invading the Ivory Coast."

She waited the beat.

There didn't seem to be a punch line.

"The Ivory Coast?" she gave a nudge for more information.

"Yeah."

"The country?" She'd heard of it, but that was the extent of her knowledge. Give her a map, and there was still no chance she'd be able to track it down. On the bottom side of the big bump beside Ghana? Or was it down the coast toward the Congo?

"Yep." Tom and Dave were tag teaming her back and forth.

"And we're invading it? Tonight?"

"Sure thing."

She stared out into the dark beyond the windows. No clues… no lights. Not even running lights…which meant this probably was real and they weren't just teasing her. She reached over to turn off the switch on the tiny Christmas tree. Looking down at the LCAC's bay where the Rangers and their vehicles were parked, not one hint of light. A very small force, which probably meant a small invasion. U.S. 75th Rangers—a Special Operations invasion, the kind that never made the news.

"I'm guessing they don't know we're coming?"

"We sure hope not."

That confirmed it.

The radar screen in front of the Chief, that she could just see over his broad shoulder, was giving some heavy bounceback along the midline of the screen. Not just ships, but shoreline.

"Well," she tried to think of something witty to say as another hard wave slammed her back in her padded seat. "Don't that beat all," was as much as she could manage.

Chapter 3

*S*ly *Stowell grinned. He* kept it under his visor, but he liked getting a piece of his own back after she'd laughed at him. Chiefs were supposed to be on the same side—no matter what their department was.

Being the backbone of the Navy wasn't a kid's game. The enlisted looked up to CPOs for guidance, and the officers needed someone who actually knew how to get things done. And just because she had "Steward" after the "Chief" rather than "Petty Officer" shouldn't matter either.

He could hear the Charleston in her voice. Southern girl. Had a laugh that sounded right down home. Who knew they built women like her, knockout redhead with a proper accent and a Chief besides. Though he did wonder about her. Some Chiefs who wore the silver rather than the gold on their insignia were more trouble than they were worth.

And not knowing to expect the Rangers on this ship? Something seriously weird about that. The *Peleliu* was no longer a standard ops ship. No Marine Expeditionary Unit aboard.

Special Forces had taken her over and the woman didn't know. Was there a reason?

Maybe she was too dense to remember her briefing?

Or had some shore-side doofus not thought it a necessary part of her briefing. He hoped to hell that she at least had the necessary security clearance. That alone was enough reason to keep her in the dark until he knew more about her.

The other reason he'd been keeping his own mouth mostly shut was that she'd peg him North Carolina right off; western NC. And she was a steward—in charge of the mess—which meant nothing but trouble to a boy from Lexington. His hometown had the best barbeque on the planet, whereas being from Charleston she would put all sorts of strange things in her sauce that were flat out wrong. Wouldn't that start a whole debate.

Stop thinking about the pretty lady! He had to stay sharp.

It wasn't often that you flew an LCAC blind—at night and running blacked out. He had no way to anticipate the waves that were slapping them around. He didn't dare risk the forward lights; they would be visible for miles if he kicked on the big floods.

So he was trusting to night vision. Problem was that looking at the world by infrared night vision made all the water look the same—too little temperature variation. Reaching land would be a relief even if that was where the shit was gonna hit the fan.

He saw a slight shimmer aloft in infrared—heat signatures in his night-vision gear—there and gone, then another. One to port, two to starboard, another to port. They showed up even less on his radar. The stealth helicopters of SOAR's 5D company were starting to gather around him. They traveled far faster than he did, so they'd left the ship later, timing their arrival to match his approach to the shore.

The woman had recovered and was asking the guys something else. He tuned back into the conversation as Dave said, "He's Sly."

"Yeah, I'll bet." She didn't get that really was his name. His dad always joked that he'd been named for Sylvester the cartoon cat. Mama just rolled her eyes at that, but never offered any other explanation.

"No, he's—"

"Two minutes out," he cut Dave off. He bumped them up another ten knots; now it got interesting.

"Weapons free."

He heard the soft, "Oh darn!" from the steward. If nothing else proved she was a lady from the South, that curse cemented it. She might be pushy, but she was a cook—her knowledge of battle probably wouldn't fill a teapot. He finally took pity on her. Teasing was fine, but you didn't scare a Chief, no matter how ditzy a one.

"My name is Sly Stowell," he offered. "What's yours?"

"Gail. Gail Miller," she was doing a fair job of straightening out her voice control though the nerves still showed through. Clearly didn't comprehend what they were headed into or she'd probably be weeping in the corner.

"Well, Gail Miller," nice name. It fit her somehow. Implied she was stronger than she appeared.

Maybe.

"The Ivory Coast is having a really rough set of elections and we're going in to clear out the U.S. Embassy in downtown Abidjan. All U.S. personnel were pulled inside the walls this morning, but they couldn't get them to the airport. They're surrounded now and the local militia is moving in on them. Nowhere near enough helicopters in the area to evac them all, so they showed some sense and called in the Navy."

"Anchors aweigh," she'd gotten control of her voice back. *Well done, Chief.* Some hope for her yet.

"We're not alone out here. There's a six-helicopter escort on us that you can't see. They're the 5D, the very best on the planet. So, hang tight in your seat and we should be in and out in thirty minutes."

# # #

Hang onto her seat? Gail was already white-knuckling it. Her last time in battle had been a dozen years ago at Battle Stations—the seventh week of boot camp. Which meant…never.

She should never have climbed aboard. They weren't even Marine Corps.

Invading a foreign country with an LCAC and a team of U.S. Rangers with a bunch of helicopters flying alongside?

The next piece registered.

"The 5D?" it came out as more of a squeak than a question. As in the Army's 160th Special Operations Aviation Regiment? They were the best helicopter pilots on the planet. And the scariest. That might explain the intermittent contacts on his radar. But they should have shown up clearly…unless…no. Not possible. Stealth birds only existed in bin Laden compound-style raids and fairy tales. Didn't they?

"That's them in all their glory," Sly was loosening up and she could hear he was a Southern boy as well, overlaid by a lot of Navy. It made her feel better for no reason that was in any way rational.

The 5th-battalion, D-company of SOAR were rumored to be the very best of the whole 160th. They always drew the ugliest assignments and then apparently pulled a lot of them off; rumors said all of them, but nobody was that good. Hell, it was only rumor that said they even existed. The 5D had taken on some kind of mythical status in the U.S. military ethos.

"Where are…" she didn't even bother to finish the question.

The place the helicopters had come from would have been the top deck of her new ship. She hadn't seen them being serviced after a day of operations, as she had believed when she approached the *Peleliu.* The helos were being prepared for a night operation.

This night operation. The one even now busting her behind as they skidded over waves and flew through the dark.

Gail would certainly make sure that she would never again go for a ride when there was any real wave action. Maybe if she closed her eyes and clicked her heels three times, she'd merely be on the small unit riverine craft with a bunch of surly Marines. At least that she understood.

She'd signed up to cook for a couple thousand Marine Corps and Navy personnel. And she was suddenly inside some kind of black ops outfit. What in the name of Father Christmas was the *Peleliu* really doing?

"Harbor in ten," Sly spoke and hammered forward the control stick. The roar didn't increase, but once more her helmet was slapped against the window close behind her as the twin fans on the stern pitched more sharply and threw the hovercraft forward.

Between one eyeblink and the next there were the lights ashore.

"Hope nobody's out night fishing," Tom offered wryly as they skidded over the wavetops. "Contact in five, four, three, two…"

And the boat was shooting up a long waterway with piers and ships to one side and a long, low shoreline to the other.

"Continue straight for three kilometers then a hard right to a course of sixty-five northeast," Tom said casually.

Gail looked down at the speed gauge that she'd picked out earlier; they were going close to a hundred knots. At a hundred and seventy kilometers an hour, three of them went by very fast.

She kept an eye out on the ships moored to starboard. Nothing fast. Have to be an ocean racer or another hovercraft to chase them. All she saw were the usual crappy rust-bucket tramp steamers that serviced such ports of call.

"Hang on!" Sly called over the PA. She could hear it both in her earphones inside her helmet as well as echoing over the boat. She couldn't hold on any harder.

Sly didn't slow down the boat. Instead he whipped the wheel to the side. The LCAC spun on its axis like a mad rollercoaster combined with one of those whirling teacup rides. In a heartbeat they were moving backwards at full speed. The two giant fans were still blowing hard, but the stern was now aimed in the direction of motion.

Bang! went her helmet as the boat's forward progress slowed in mere moments. Then Sly spun a quarter turn around and they were roaring off beneath a pair of bridges and gaining speed at a course ninety degrees from their prior one. Not a ship on the planet, with its keel in the water, could have made such a turn.

And, Gail suspected, not all that many LCAC pilots. There was a smoothness, a level of skill that shone from the man. Daddy had pointed out what skill looked like when a guy named Hubert had come out to excavate a vacant lot on their block for a new house. He made that backhoe dance, doing two and three compound movements at once. Her dad made sure she saw how the contractor had dovetailed all his movements.

Daddy was always doing things like that. University professor turning his daughter into a master observer. "My little Sherlock," was one of his pet names.

Color of the shirt on the man we just passed; no, don't look.

Close your eyes and describe that woman's tattoo.

They still played the game when she was home on vacation, challenging each other with more and more impossible observations. It had given them something to talk about through the teen years when there was no way she was sharing her feelings or anything else about her life.

It let her see that Chief Petty Officer Sly Stowell drove his hovercraft the same way that Hubert drove his backhoe; like it was art.

The hovercraft felt as if it constantly searched for an excuse to skitter madly about—yet with Sly at the controls, it flew dead clean. The U.S. Navy was invading the Ivory Coast and they'd chosen him to drive the only water craft in the attack. His behind might be wet, but his skills were clearly among the elite.

On top of that, if the *Peleliu* was indeed living some secret identity, only the very best would be aboard.

Which inevitably led back to her earlier question: What in the name of all that was holy was she doing here? The pieces of that puzzle eluded her completely.

Three kilometers and one minute later, they were on the far side of Abidjan harbor. If there were any vessels coming for them, they'd be moving far slower. She saw limited car traffic ashore and on the bridges, but none on the water.

"Hang a left here," Tom spoke again.

"Okay," Sly turned and finally slowed, though the roar of the four massive gas turbine engines didn't ease.

They were so steady about it all that she wanted to reach forward and bang their helmets together—if she could unclench her hands from the seat.

# # #

Sly hit the beach at thirty knots. They roared up over the sand and flattened a row of low bushes. Recon had said no barriers over three feet in height along their route, which had better be true. He could clear four feet, but anything more and he was likely to high-center on it and finish out his life as a teeter-totter.

"Left on the Boulevard de France."

"Roger that," Sly turned onto the two-lane highway that followed the shoreline. The shoulders were dotted with widely spaced palms. Even with his elevated view from the control cockpit he still couldn't see many lights to either side. Whatever troubles this city was having today, the electricity had clearly been one of the early victims.

"After that, the second turn will be coming up on your right."

Tom was playing it perfectly, good man. They'd worked out every inch of this route in the planning session six hours ago. But his navigator was making it sound like they were out for a Sunday drive to tease their unexpected passenger.

Sly felt as if he was flying at a whole different level with her aboard; a better one. He hit the Boulevard. Rather than slowing for the turn, he once again slewed the tail backwards to make the turn clean. And he nailed it, dead down the two-lane road without bouncing off the trees to either side. Her presence was now lending him a focus rather than distracting him.

Damned show off!

He grinned.

Well, even if the girl didn't know enough to be impressed, he could see Dave and Tom were appreciating the ride. He'd wager that the Rangers down in their holes wouldn't be though. That focused his thoughts back on the job at hand.

A night bus was approaching them from the opposite direction. No way to hear the horn that he was sure was blaring, but he could well imagine how wide the driver's eyes were as the front of the bus slammed down from heavy braking. At fifteen meters wide, the LCAC took up both lanes and the shoulders of the shoreline boulevard.

A dozen meters from running over the stopped bus—

"Turn right onto the seventh fairway. It's a par four, watch out for the water trap by the green."

He flattened a couple of trees as he broke onto the fairway.

"Dear God in the mornin', spare me from such men," Gail muttered with an overly thick Southern accent; he could hear the laugh in her voice. She'd clearly caught on to what they were doing to her.

Maybe she wasn't a ditz. Maybe she'd just been messing with him too.

Damn!

If that was true he could actually get to like her…even if she was from Charleston.

"Cut north to the third fairway…now!"

Sly slewed north then back west.

"This is a par five, but since you came into the middle of the fairway, we're only going to give you three strokes."

"Two," Gail countered Tom's ruling. "If he's any good, he can do it in two."

"At the green, jog left to pick up the fourth."

"No divots, Chief."

"Goddamn it!" He was maneuvering a thirty-meter long, eighty-ton hovercraft with forty tons of gear and Rangers aboard over a golf course. He didn't have time to laugh.

He actually rode the edge of the rise on the third green to help him bank through the turn and left it undamaged except for a huge puff of sand out of the sand trap. He drove up the fourth fairway, slowing down in the dogleg and turning right through a gap in the trees when the fairway turned left.

"Ooooo!" Gail moaned as if in the agony of disappointment. "Into the rough. Drop and a one-stroke penalty. Gonna be tough to get your birdie now, Chief."

He was fifty meters from the tall concrete wall around the U.S. embassy when a missile roared out of the dark and shattered a ten-meter section of it.

That was SOAR; always right on schedule.

He noticed that Gail didn't have a word to say about that.

Through the gap in the wall he spotted one of SOAR's Little Birds easing to a hover over the embassy. Four men slid down fast-ropes onto the roof. That would be Michael and three other Delta Force operators. Like Lieutenant Barstowe in the Rangers, Michael was an officer who led from all the way out front, something Sly could definitely respect.

He eased the LCAC up to the rubble and lowered the hovercraft to the ground. They settled onto the grass, his bow gate pointed directly at the breach in the embassy's concrete wall.

In moments they had the gate lowered. U.S. Rangers and the three M-ATVs made short work of entering the compound.

"C'mon people," he muttered.

A crowd began to pour out of the compound. A dribble at first, but then a thick press of them. Men, women, some children. A lot of briefcases, some suitcases, and more than one idiot with a bag of golf clubs.

"Nika?" he called over the headset intercom. In addition to being loadmaster and port-side spotter, she was also his port-side gunner. Always good to remind her that he had his eye on his crew.

"Here, Chief."

"You have my permission to shoot the next asshole who is trying to rescue his golf game." And to remind his crew that he trusted them implicitly.

"Roger that, Chief."

Then she unleashed a dozen half-inch rounds against a still upright section of the wall. It didn't care, except for some chips in the surface. But the harsh bark of the M2 Browning machine gun put a whole lot of hustle into people moving toward his craft.

Well played. He'd have to remember that in the debrief.

Then it happened. They'd been waiting for it, expecting it ever since the ambassador had called in a panic at two this afternoon.

The top floor of the U.S. embassy bloomed up in a ball of fire. Someone outside the front gate had just fired something big at the building. Not just a rocket-propelled grenade. That had to be a two-inch shell at least to make that kind of fireball. He hoped to god Michael and his boys had already left the top floor on their way down from the roof.

It had been something major.

Tank maybe.

But that's why they had SOAR along.

Even so, he wished the Rangers would hurry the hell up.

# # #

Gail looked at the three men seated with their backs to her in disbelief. They were just sitting there, doing nothing!

The embassy was burning and they were—

A lance of green fire slashed down from the heavens.

Right. She'd momentarily forgotten about the helicopters.

Not just helicopters. The 5D.

Their M134 miniguns were cutting up whoever had just attacked the embassy. Searchlights were flickering on, aimed upward to find the helicopters—which explained why they'd waited for nightfall. And the lights were being shot out just as fast as they appeared.

For an instant she saw a tiny helicopter silhouetted against the embassy and moving fast. It couldn't be more than five feet off the ground and it was laying down a hail of fire that lit the night sky. Then the nose jerked up and it disappeared once more into the darkness.

Embassy personnel were, finally, scrambling over the rubble of the wall as fast as they could. Golf bags, suitcases, even framed pictures for crying out loud, were now scattered far and wide as the personnel ran for their lives.

A small force of embassy Marines worked rearguard on the civilians. Deep in the compound, she could see the three Rangers' vehicles rushing about—a near constant hail of fire from their gun turrets. Combat medics were out on the ground, gathering up the fallen and loading them aboard the two ambulances.

She heard the harsh bark of Nika's half-inch gun. She was fighting a battle off to the port side.

Then why weren't the bad guys also over—

Gail spun to look out the starboard side.

"Chief, due east."

A pickup truck with a heavy machine gun mounted on its bed was rounding the outside corner of the embassy perimeter wall.

He spun to look out his side window and didn't waste any time swearing. "Get down!" he shouted at her.

She popped her seatbelt and dove to the deck as gunfire poured against the starboard side glass. It didn't shatter, not right away, which gave all of the guys time to get down as well.

"*Vengeance*," Sly called over the radio. "This is the LCAC. Trouble due east."

"Roger," a woman's voice answered. "I suppose you want the Army to clean it up for you?"

Another round of gunfire shattered the starboard window and blew out the port one for good measure, showering them with broken chunks of polycarbonate the size of her hand.

"That would be nice."

Gail wondered what the heck was wrong with these people. Even as she wondered, she saw a single missile streak down out of the dark from somewhere high above. Since she didn't dare look out the window, she'd shifted so that she could watch the radar screen. She could see the missile on the radar sweep, but not the much larger helicopter that must have fired it.

Another point in favor of her stealth theory no matter how bizarre it might be.

The answering explosion on the ground was impressive.

"Hole in one. Anything else, Chief?" the woman again. Gail had heard rumors of women flying for SOAR, but that's how everything was with SOAR, rumors.

Sly looked up and did a quick scan around before brushing the glass out of his seat and sitting back down. "We're good, unless you have the number of a local window replacement company."

"On your own there. Here come your Rangers."

Gail edged back up to her seat. Now that the glass was gone, she was far more exposed, but she felt foolish crouching on the floor while the others sat up.

Sly looked back at her for a long moment, but she couldn't read his expression behind his lowered visor. He had one of those rigs that projected most of the information he needed on the inside of his visor. That was another thing she'd like to try someday. Her own visor was a piece of clear plastic that might stop a .22 round if it was having a slow day.

The last of the Rangers were back at the wall. They were driving their vehicles up the hovercraft's forward ramp, shooing civilians to the sides of the deck as they loaded the heavy vehicles.

The battle was still primarily concentrated on the far side of the building. Four soldiers remained on the ground of the embassy compound even as Tom was raising the LCAC's front gate. She was about to point them out when a tiny helicopter swooped down among them.

Definitely no radar image.

Too far away to see more than a silhouette, but it confirmed her theory.

Her theory about something there was no way she was cleared to know.

Stealth was one of SOAR's most closely guarded secrets.

The bird never came to a full stop, or landed. All it did was hesitate at ground level and in moments the four soldiers were sitting on the bench seats, two to either side. Even as they lifted back into the darkness, she could see the men sitting on the bench using their elevated position to fire their rifles down into the hostiles.

She'd never seen a maneuver quite like it.

She was also fairly sure they hadn't been wearing any packs when they landed on the rooftop. Now all four were heavily-laden. What had they fetched while inside?

If she wasn't cleared to know about stealth, whatever they had was something she really, really wasn't cleared to know.

Gail tried to smell the night air, but all she got was hot exhaust fumes and the smell of the burning truck nearby. She kept checking, as did Chief Stowell, but no one else had tried to come around that corner.

The hovercraft was on the move and back over the third fairway before Sly spoke.

"Nice spotting on that truck. Good eye, Chief Miller."

"Got two of 'em, Chief Stowell."

"You play golf?" He headed them back onto the seventh fairway.

Gail looked back at the burning building behind them. No more gunfire or missiles from the sky. But she could feel the 5D out there somewhere, watching over them—invisibly—as the hovercraft picked up speed and headed back for the Boulevard de France and the harbor.

Their protection was the only reason she could breathe.

"Twenty bucks a hole, Chief."

"Damn! Way too rich for my blood." They descended the beach, hit the water, and then they were speeding through the harbor once more at over seventy knots.

Even though she'd bet the Chief wouldn't take the turn so fast with all of the people on the deck below, she refastened her seatbelt.

Too rich for his blood, huh?

"Wait 'til you try my cooking."

He laughed. A real one. As good as his smile.

Chapter 4

G*ail ended up dripping* wet by the time she followed Sly onto the *Peleliu.*

With the windows shot out, the LCAC's reentry into the *Peleliu's* Well Deck and the resulting solid wall of spray had blown right into the control room and soaked them all.

They were last ashore, the embassy staff had already been escorted up to the Flight Deck for transport to the carrier.

Gail desperately wanted to go find her duffle and fresh clothes.

Instead, Sly Stowell tossed her a towel and led her up onto the Flight Deck, six or seven ladderways above the Well Deck. The darkness was thick over most of the *Peleliu's* deck and the stars shone brightly high above them. A waning quarter moon was nosing up out of the sea like a mystical Moby Dick.

At the far end of the Flight Deck a pair of massive Marine Corps Super Stallion helicopters were actively loading the embassy staff to ferry them over to the aircraft carrier steaming fifty kilometers farther west. She could see two more of the monsters hovering off the stern waiting their turns.

SOAR's helicopters were already parked along the deck, covered in nylon shrouds as dark as the night which hid their shapes.

She could tell there were small and medium ones, Little Birds and Black Hawks.

"What's with the camo on the birds? Oh, never mind."

"You don't leave Special Ops helicopters out in plain sight when there are civilians aboard."

"Not Special Ops. Stealth. I figured that out earlier," she saw his surprise. "Didn't show up on your radar, Chief, when I was looking right at them. I'm just having trouble believing it."

The word finally sunk in and she ground to a halt. Planted her feet solidly; it felt as if the deck was thrashing about in an attempt to dump her overboard. The cataloging part of her brain saw that the deck was rock stable to the moonlit horizon.

Okay, she was the one at sea.

Stealth?

Her request for a transfer to a ship, any ship, unexpectedly granted. And at whirlwind speed. Navy Personnel Command was a notoriously lethargic operation. Yet within two days of putting in a transfer she'd received orders for immediate travel halfway around the world.

As if her name had been on some watch list.

Overload!

Something was going on behind the scenes and she had no idea what.

Tilt!

"Chief Stowell," her brain had just completely and totally crashed. "I really need to dry off and get some rack time if I want to be ready for my first breakfast service."

"Breakfast was four hours ago. I'll take you to lunch after the debriefing."

Debriefing? Her? Okay, sure. Whatever.

Gail checked her watch, close enough to midnight to not make any real difference. She sighed and gave in enough to ask the question.

"Okay, what's the darn joke?"

"The joke?" Stowell just watched her like she was some sort of child. His handsome face lit by the soft red glow from the night-time flight operations at the far end of the Flight Deck. The pale moon beyond his shoulder was now swollen large enough out of the ocean to give Captain Ahab conniption fits.

She felt a strong empathy for Ahab at the moment. Chief Steward Gail Miller was definitely losing her mind.

Sly Stowell looked at her as if she were dense.

"I sign up for Marines and I get Special Ops. Instead of the usual Super Stallion," she waved a hand toward the departing helos at the far end of the Flight Deck, "and a couple of Cobra helicopters on this LHA ship, I get the stealth arm of SOAR. Yesterday I'd have given the 5D a fifty-fifty chance of being a myth, a boogie man created by Psy Ops to scare the enemy. Tonight I watched them fly. And those guys who hit the roof from the helo, there was something strange about them too that I haven't quite figured out yet. So how about some explaining?"

He rubbed his chin as he inspected her, "You figured all that?"

"Not an idiot, Chief."

"No, I can see that now."

"Oh, *now*. Fine." So that had been his first impression of her? Not exactly what a girl wanted to project.

"The Christmas tree."

"What?"

"'Oh!'" he made his voice high and squeaky. "'What a cute little Christmas tree!'"

She laughed, "Okay, I deserved that. Just didn't want to brush up your ego about how cool your ship looked. I'd like a real tour sometime."

"What's your clearance?"

"Probably better than yours," she shot back as a piece clicked into place. Daddy spent a lot of time in D.C. consulting when he wasn't teaching, probably for the Navy—naval tactics being his specialty. Mama also taught at the Citadel, so the Naval

Personnel Command would know a lot about her too; about all three of them. Duh!

Sly looked offended.

"Navy Chief of Staff visits the SUBASE and guess which chef pulls meal service during the meetings." She made a curtsey as if wearing a pinafore and not khakis and a blouse that should have been washed days ago and were still far from dry. She did her best to not let it sound as if she'd only just figured out her own security clearance.

"Now talk."

Sly Stowell grunted at that.

Maybe if she just threw the man overboard she'd get some answers.

"The USS *Peleliu* has been reassigned," he explained, perhaps reading her intent and deciding to cooperate at long last. "We support SOAR and Special Operation Forces on *ad hoc* missions. There's not a single Marine Corps jarhead aboard. What you've got here are Rangers and Delta."

"Delta?" She'd never seen a Delta Force operator up close. Once or twice they'd pass through one of her messes—you could tell because they wore longer hair or beards and always sat by themselves. Also, no uniforms, and no one ever sat near them. They'd be on some mission that no one knew anything about and then, like ghosts, they'd be gone again.

"The four men who used a racing helicopter as a shooting platform…"

"Delta," he confirmed.

When she didn't respond—couldn't respond—he continued.

"They all work in a flipped clock world. The 5D flies at night and sleeps during the day. Navy is still standing three watches, but midrats are at noon, not midnight. Still need rations for those few Navy folk working the quiet watches."

Well, being Navy was about being flexible and she typically worked deep inside the ship, so what the sun was doing in the sky didn't affect her all that much. Heck, she'd probably see more of it this way—don't see a whole lot of sunlight when you're busy from breakfast prep through dinner service every day.

Sly led her into the tower of the communications structure, knocked on a door that bore the simple sign "Ramis," then held it open for her when they were called to enter.

His enigmatic smile should have warned her.

She was still figuratively wet behind the ears and literally dripping from her pant cuffs when she met her new commanding officer. An event for which one CPO Sly Stowell was definitely going to suffer later. At least some of her hair was dry from being inside her helmet.

The Lieutenant Commander's office still showed evidence of being a former ready room, but had been converted to a spacious office with enough furniture that a mission debrief could indeed be held here. Two couches and a half-dozen chairs were bolted down, as well as assorted bench seats and a few loose chairs. The wall sported a collection of what she assumed were the commanding officer's succession of commands in order. This boat was clearly the jewel of the series, an aging craft technically past retirement, but now repurposed for SOAR.

Lieutenant Commander Boyd Ramis was a tall man, running a little thick around the middle and graying at the temples. He came out from behind his desk to greet her and offer a stout handshake that she did her best to return.

"Chief Miller. I appear to have met your gear before I met my Chief Steward," he nodded toward a corner of the room where her pack and knife case had been tucked.

She fought the heat rising to her cheeks, "I'm sorry, sir. Had never been on an LCAC before and was glad of the opportunity. Chief Stowell was kind enough to let me ride along as an observer."

LCDR Ramis looked unperturbed by her transgression, which struck her as odd. There wasn't a single commander in her past that wouldn't take her to task for it. She'd simply followed her whim, which hadn't been very Navy of her.

"Was it an interesting journey?"

She shot a surprised glance at Sly.

He read the question and offered a non-committal shrug. LCDR Ramis' attitude wasn't any real surprise to the Chief Petty Officer.

Gail struggled for a straight answer, "It was very…educational, sir."

"Good. All in favor of having a well-rounded staff."

"First time invading a foreign country as well?" Sly was being, well, sly. So much for being kind. She didn't need to feel a poke in her ribs to know when it was happening.

"Well, I *had* thought you *might* be doing something exciting," she made a bet with herself about the LCDR's command style and turned back to him as Sly opened his mouth to protest. "Honestly, sir, all they did was play a little golf with a hundred-ton club and park outside a hole in the wall for a little bit. They weren't even the ones to put the hole there in the first place."

"No, that would have been me," a tall woman entered the office. A voice Gail recognized from the radio chatter, what little there'd been of it. "Chief Warrant Lola Maloney at your service." She was taller than Gail, almost as tall as Sly, slender and with mahogany hair that fluttered down around her face. Long hair to her shoulders. If there was anything in the U.S. military that indicated Special Forces, it was non-standard hair.

Others drifted in and were introduced. Lead pilots—several of them women, air mission commander and his daughter—which was pretty weird, the lieutenant of the Ranger company again wearing his Santa hat—who had surprisingly little swagger for being a Ranger. And then she saw why. She almost missed the man who came in beside him.

He was just her own height, not a big man either, blond hair down to his jaw line, but he moved so softly. It was as if he wasn't there. He looked…amused that she saw him at all though there were under a dozen people in Ramis' spacious office.

"Colonel Gibson," he introduced himself.

"Delta," she breathed out. His presence was simply so powerful that there was no question.

"Please to meet you, Delta." He said it with a straight face. He looked familiar, but she couldn't place him—which was unusual for her.

She almost had it when a short redheaded woman punched him on the arm.

"Duh, Michael! You're the one who's Delta. She's just in shell shock. And don't go getting all mushy on her, Sly will get jealous. Trisha O'Malley, hi!" Her fine-fingered handshake was tougher than any of the guys.

"Gail Miller," she managed. *Sly would be jealous?* Of what!

Gail glanced over at him. He was busy scowling down at Trisha.

"Whoops!" the redhead shrugged. "You'll discover that I have a big mouth. Look forward to trying your food anyway." And she scooted off to tease the dark-skinned teenager who was as tall as she was and clearly still headed upward.

Gail tried to decide if her head was hurting from the whirlwind of what was happening around her or from the unexpected jarring aboard the hovercraft. Yes was the obvious, all-encompassing answer.

Would it be better if she just went with the flow of mayhem? Probably.

Could she? Not a chance.

She hadn't attended many mission debriefings, none at all since Basic Training, but she couldn't imagine they were often like this one.

There was as many jokes as facts.

Serious one moment as they reviewed estimated body counts among the attackers and injured Americans removed from the compound by the ambulances, to once again teasing Sly about his "golf game."

Her own analysis of the attack against the LCAC drew interest. Her observations of an attack as coming from one side, implying an attack from the other had Sly studying her closely and the silent D-boy nodding. Her explanation had prompted a discussion of tactics on how to avoid a recurrence. As Sly considered a permanent spotter to be added to the control-room jump seat, he did note that it had been getting stuffy in there anyway and the fresh air through the missing windows had been nice.

Gail liked the way the conversation rolled back and forth. There was no question of competence here, these people were all the very best at what they did.

Even LCDR Ramis filled his role exceptionally well. A more ambitious or forceful commander would have been a problem. Ramis was a perfect facilitator, giving this elite team enough room to operate in their own specialty with all of their odd quirks out in the open, yet coordinate it with those around them. It was difficult to imagine him commanding a standard helicopter carrier with a full Marine Corps Expeditionary Unit—not enough of a hard-core commander in him, but this appeared to work well.

"Well," Ramis gave a *that's that,* wrap-up tone to his voice. "It seems that your plan came off without any real hitch, Michael. Well done. Very well done indeed."

The Delta operator hadn't spoken once throughout the entire debrief, but everyone was nodding. He'd gone invisible on her during the meeting, somehow fading away for most of it until she'd forgotten he was there. She could see by his eyes that he had missed absolutely nothing, and felt no need to embellish what the others said except for that one confirming nod. So that's what praise for a D-boy felt like? Pretty good.

Sly Stowell, seated on the couch beside her, showed that same sharp awareness and tracking of every detail.

And unlike the D-boy, the Chief hadn't had the decency to fade away from her awareness even in the slightest.

Sly would be jealous?

There was nothing to be jealous of. Was there?

Gail wanted to smack herself sensible, but didn't see it happening anytime soon. Not until she got some sleep at least… and a little distance from the Chief. There was too much new information slamming into her head and she still hadn't seen her new kitchen or met any of the staff.

"Chief Miller?"

Sly Stowell was standing in front of her. Others were already filing out of the room. He'd extended one hand to help her up off the couch holding her duffle with the other. Not thinking, she took his hand, and felt the power of his grasp. His grip wasn't hard or crushing, but it was so firm and solid that there could be no doubt of his strength. He was a far more powerful man than he looked at first glance.

She was tired enough to let herself appreciate his assistance for a moment longer than was necessary. His weren't a cook's hands. A cook's were strong, yes, but soft from being so constantly wet and marked by various small nicks and cuts, calloused only against minor burns and the grip on a chef's knife. Sly's were hands that belonged to a career Navy man: rough, muscular, ready for any task.

With a slight squeeze of thanks for his assistance, she let go and reached to take her gear.

Sly swung the straps of her duffle over his shoulder as if it weighed ounces instead of the tons she always imagined.

Gathering up her knife case, she waved for him to lead the way, especially as she had no idea where she was going.

At least she'd finally dried out in the warmth of Ramis' office.

# # #

Sly led her to her quarters, "02 Deck, Frame 8, 3-L. Odd number means you're to starboard side. L is living space."

"Knew that."

"Figures," Sly muttered to himself. She'd mentioned being ashore for two years, but she still had that fact. Clearly she had a mind like a steel trap despite his initial estimates of her intelligence.

"Ages ago," she grinned at him. "I thought that neuron died while cooking for a bunch of brown-bagging bubbleheads."

Funny.

Funny and cute.

Funny and gorgeous.

Don't go there, Chief!

Leave it to the submarine corps to ignore a pretty chef and bring their own lunches from home when ashore. If he had a billet with a chef who looked like her, he'd never miss a single meal.

Though he was still chagrined that she'd spotted the attacking truck at the U.S. embassy before he had. He'd been estimating payload and balance as he counted how many people were on-loading at the embassy. An extra twenty tons of people—minus their golf clubs—his load capacity was still okay on top of the Rangers and forty tons of M-ATVs.

Right until someone started shooting up his side window.

Her quarters were standard Navy issue, for an officer. Without a full complement of Marines aboard and SOAR doing their own aircraft maintenance, the ship was running with one third of their standard Navy crew. It opened up spaces to allow the new Chief Steward to have a private cabin among the command berths. She'd still rank her own cabin, just not usually in officer country. His own quarters were 3-80-2-L, way at the back-end of the next deck down, close up against the Hangar Deck that occupied the aft half of the boat at this level.

She had a solo bunk, a couple drawers, and a narrow closet. He had the low bunk in a two-stack berth, but because they were running light, he had the two-stack to himself. Pretty luxurious by any Chief Petty Officer standards. He'd definitely miss the *Peleliu* when she finally went out of service.

"Don't you have somewhere you have to be?"

"Trying to get rid of me?" he made it a joke and was a little surprised that he didn't want to go.

"Why? Would it work if I was?" She made it a tease.

Her smile made him laugh. "Not if you're saying it like that, ma'am. Besides, Dave and Tom will see to the windows, probably already have. Glad to show you about, Chief." And he was. More than that. He didn't want anyone else doing it.

It wasn't some possessive thing, no matter what crap Trisha O'Malley was slinging his way. It was that he liked watching Gail Miller as she discovered things.

There was no wide-eyed innocence. Instead, she was drinking everything in as if she could never be satisfied. What she'd observed and recalled of their attack on the embassy had been staggering. Everything cataloged and archived in the very neatly organized mind he was discovering beneath that silky red hair.

Her first battle, probably since Basic, and she'd climbed back up into her seat as soon as he had—he'd expected her to be cowering on the deck and then need a post-battle counselor to coax her out of the LCAC.

Woman had sat right back up and resumed her self-appointed lookout duty. Damn!

She waved for him to lead the way, keeping the small case black case with her.

Special spices? No, knives.

A woman who fetched along her own knives. Just added to the fine image she was already painting right in front of him.

Chapter 5

*W*e're only running the officer's Wardroom Mess and the Chief's for all the ship's personnel. You can run both from a common galley so you'll be getting less of a workout than back when we were fully crewed," Sly informed her. "Normally, you'd have four messes and two galleys spread across four decks."

Gail wasn't sure whether it was normal for one Chief to tour another through the ship, but she wasn't complaining. The *Peleliu* was so big that once she was lost they might never find her again.

"Wardroom Mess is on the 02 Deck forward with the Chief's Mess directly below on 03. That's where your main galley kitchen is. The 04 and 05 galley and messes for the Marines are all shut down."

Well that simplified things somewhat. To run a double galley you needed to have an assistant that you knew and trusted, whereas she hadn't even met her staff yet. Somehow she'd become snarled up with the Special Operations crews though, which had made her arrival interesting even if it wasn't likely to ever affect her again.

She'd also met Chief Sly Stowell. Mr. Model Navy clearly commanded immense respect, even from the elite forces aboard. She'd seen it clearly at the debriefing and now in the passageways as people greeted him or made way depending on their rank.

"However, down the 04 and 05 decks are your pantry, cold stores, butcher shop, baker's space, and all that. I'll show you all the shortcuts."

Shortcuts? Gail's last ship had included four decks, total. This beast had eight, not counting the four or five of the Communications Superstructure. The *Peleliu* was twice as wide, twice as long, and ten times the displacement tonnage. The frigate USS *James Reuben* had barely two hundred personnel. Gail had been both excited and daunted by the three thousand she'd expected to be serving aboard her new ship. That there *only* six hundred aboard was both a relief and a challenge. It might not be the same monster task, but bringing her A-game was still going to be her main goal.

"And here's your new crew."

Gail was shocked, because she hadn't smelled it first.

A galley should intrigue, tease, entice.

She stood in the doorway to the galley and mainly smelled sweat and grease. What she saw was frying burgers and dogs. No scent of even the sharp bite of vinegar on slaw though she could see it was already set in large serving pans.

One of the crew had a cigarette dangling from the corner of his lips as he leaned over to inspect a vast soup pot.

"Put that out now, sailor!" she snapped without even thinking.

The man stood up slowly and turned to her. He wore sloppy khakis and an apron that might have once been white. A long, slow, toe-to-head inspection made him smirk.

"You're the new chief, huh?"

"I am."

The man, who looked like he'd spent far too much of his life indulging in the cooking spirits, took his cigarette out of his mouth, inspected it carefully, and then took another deliberate puff.

"On report, sailor!" she snapped. Not how she wanted to meet her crew.

He turned to face Sly who had remained silent beside her, "Hey, Sly."

"Hey, Vic."

"Does she think I actually give a flying rat's ass what some bitch thinks?"

Sly started to speak.

Gail cut him off.

She stepped up toe-to-toe with the man who outweighed her by at least twice. She took the cigarette from his lips and tossed it into the cleanup sink.

"You and you," she pointed at two of the staff who didn't look to be doing much when she walked in and had remained frozen in her peripheral vision to watch the show, "you will escort this man to the brig. You, sailor, are under arrest for insubordination to a superior rank."

He laughed a steamy stale tobacco-laced breath right in her face. "I'm the outgoing Chief Stew. Same damned rank. Can't do shit to me, lady."

"You think?" she tapped her insignia, "this says I can. This is my mess now and you're no longer welcome." She finally turned from the belligerent idiot and faced the two she'd indicated earlier. "Get him out of here and into lockup, now!"

She waited until, with soft-voiced apologies, they escorted the man out. He looked pissed as hell and she didn't give a damn.

"Chief, I—"

She cut off whatever Sly had been about to say.

"My crew now, Chief. I'd appreciate it if you backed off."

# # #

And Sly did, but he stayed close, hanging just outside the galley in the still unoccupied mess. There were only three or four people at the various tables, playing cards or reading a book while they waited for the start of service. From here he could hear what was happening in the galley but not be seen.

Vic had always been a misogynistic asshole. He'd lost rank twice before he learned to keep his hands to himself; instead, he'd learned how to ride the legal edge of sexual harassment, barely. Twenty-five years in had been twenty-four too long. But he'd kept everyone fed and knew when to keep his trap shut—except about women.

"Y'all," he heard her voice clearly from his position out in the passage—he liked that *Y'all,* sounded good on her—"have thirty seconds to find a clean apron and a chef's hat. After that, anyone who is found without their hair properly covered had better find another ship. Then I want everyone at the scrub sink, right up to your elbows for a minimum of twenty seconds under hot water. Are we clear?"

There was a brief silence.

"Now!"

At the sound of her shout there was a sudden loud shuffle of feet inside the galley. The water started running.

Well, that was a Chief Steward Gail Miller that he hadn't met on the LCAC or in the debriefing. She'd been funny, whimsical, polite, and thoughtful. She'd also successfully baited him several times—that he knew of.

But in her own environment? It was clear she kicked ass and took no guff from any man's son. When this day had started, he hadn't expected to respect her.

"Service doesn't start for thirty minutes, why are you cooking already?" Her voice barely carried out to him though she no longer had that snap. It was more a one-to-one human question.

Didn't berate her crew except when needed. Another mark in her favor.

"Never mind. Scrape all that off the grill and then clean it. That's it. Hit it with some water to break loose the burned-on whatever that is."

A sharp sizzle erupted as cold water was sprayed on hot steel. Then the scrubbing sound of wire brushes on the griddle.

"We're starting over. Is that mixer there clean? Good. I want fifty pounds of ground chuck, four dozen eggs, a cup of dried oregano, two cups…"

She went on listing spices and quantities. Then she was adding cayenne pepper to the chowder, explaining aloud what she was doing, making everyone taste it first.

"What do you mean there's no vegetarian option?"

"Chef said—"

"You!" again that clear sense of command as she cut off whoever dared answer her, but still no harsh tone despite what must have been a building frustration. "Go find me some polenta, refried beans, green and red peppers, onions…"

Sly nodded to the two returning culinary specialists headed back from delivering Vic to the brig. "Better put some hustle on boys. It's a new world in there."

They looked at him wide-eyed and then hurried in.

"And why isn't there any music? It's Christmas, boys and girls." Moments later he heard a Christmas carol start up. She must have brought a personal player with her, probably tucked in that knife case, and patched it into the galley's audio.

"Way better," she announced as Taylor Swift began kicking out *Santa Baby*.

So, lady was into Christmas. Have to see if she was rational about it, or a loony like his family. Mama, Daddy, and the whole crowd always made a serious deal about it.

Sly spent his holiday seasons on-board ship. No gal at home. Not much to do with leave when he had it. Sly didn't even keep an apartment or bother with a car. Thirty days off a year; he'd mostly go exploring for a couple days at a time whenever they docked somewhere new. The *Peleliu* was his home and he was relieved that her life had been extended by the Night Stalkers.

His folks were always pushing him to come home for Christmas. The only one of their kids without family, and grandkids for them—it always left him feeling kinda lost. He figured to stay aboard and let those who really cared about it try for leave to get home.

Personally, the only holiday he always put in for was the end of October, the Annual Barbeque Festival in Lexington. Best barbeque on the planet. He made sure never to miss a year; hadn't since he was a snot-nosed kid of six and it was the first-ever festival—except a few times, like the speed run from Australia to the North Arabian Sea after the 9/11 attacks. All leave had been cancelled and he'd been way too pissed at Al-Qaeda to argue.

Sly wandered off. He had time to go check on the repairs to his LCAC, but this was a meal he was looking forward to.

He slid down the ladderway headed for the Well Deck.

Sly was also looking forward to learning more about Chief Gail Miller. Which, he had to admit, had to do with more than merely welcoming another sailor into the *Peleliu* fold.

It took him a while to notice what he was whistling as he arrived at his LCAC.

It's Beginning to Look a Lot Like Christmas.

He wasn't going to tell anyone that it was the Alvin and the Chipmunks version inside his head.

Chapter 6

*C*aptain wants to see you."

Gail looked up at the Seaman Second and tried to make sense of the words.

"Why?"

"Like I'd know. He's in the Officer's Mess."

"Which is where?"

The Seaman eyed her strangely.

"I've been on board for three hours, most of which I spent right here. Give me a break, sailor."

"Yes, Chief. Sorry, Chief."

She turned back to her new staff. "Take an hour." Stingy. "I'd give you two, but I think we have some catching up to do." Let them know it was to be an exception, not a habit.

They nodded, several smiled.

She wondered how long it had been since they'd felt good about reporting for kitchen duty. For all she could see, they were a good group simply in want of a little leadership, and a lot of training. *A person* needs *to feel they're learning.*

Something Daddy always said that she'd discovered to be absolutely true.

Gail considered thanking them as they filed out. She wanted to build a team, but she wanted it to be a Navy team, so she offered them a simple nod instead. Then she pulled the jack out of her music player and tucked it back into her knife case. She always cooked to music. And from Thanksgiving to Christmas, her and her Mama's favorite music was fair game. Mama was always adding the latest holiday album to their shared playlist. Pretty soon Gail would be able to go a whole season without a single repeat.

The kitchen was empty, except the Seaman Second Class who was still waiting for her. The line of big stainless-steel steam kettles the size of fifty-five gallon drums were empty. The pair of six-foot griddles were cooling off from their hot work. Burners off. Pots, pans, bowls all run through the industrial washer and tucked away secure against an unexpected sea roll.

We get a hurricane, she silently warned the crew, *you're getting peanut butter and jelly sandwiches.*

"Okay," Gail tucked away her knife case in the Chief Steward's locker and turned to the Seaman. "Lead away."

She'd been on the ship three hours and one meal—six hours and one meal if you counted the trip to the Ivory Coast.

First question that came to mind: Was she about to be thrown off?

# # #

Sly still wasn't used to eating in the Officer's Mess. When they'd off-loaded the Marines and on-boarded SOAR and the Rangers, they'd shifted around to consolidate the dining. Chief and above, SOAR's flight crews, and the top Rangers all ate in the Officer's Mess. Second class petty officers and down, SOAR line crews, and Ranger grunts shared the Crew's Mess on the deck directly below.

Delta Force, the four of them, also ate in the Officer's Mess and had staked out the two tables in the back corner, facing the entryway. Only a couple of the SOAR women comfortably crossed that invisible line from time to time. No one else.

Sly certainly didn't.

What the hell do you say to a D-boy? They couldn't talk about missions. "So, what did you guys take out of the American embassy in those packs?"

Talk about their girlfriends?

One had married the SOAR pilot, Trisha, funniest looking couple he ever saw—a six-foot D-boy who never spoke and a five-foot Irish redhead who never stopped.

Besides, Sly didn't have a girl. He'd sometimes pick up a honey for a week's leave. Or he and some cute Lieutenant might agree to leave separately, then just happen to land on the same Italian beach or Pacific Island for a week's R&R. The definition of safe, no-commitment sex—because if you got caught, you got court-martialed. What happened on the beach, stayed on the beach. Worked out for everyone.

It had been a while since he'd had one of those. When he considered doing something about that, Chief Gail Miller and that easy laugh of hers rose to mind very easily. Too easily. Getting a soft spot in his brain for a fellow Chief was not the best idea. And that was completely aside from the fact that he'd only met her this morning.

He looked around the mess for a distraction. There were a couple of lame strands of red and green bunting laced through the overhead pipes and ductwork. A big Christmas tree was tied into the corner of the space—a popup from a box, not a live one—mostly decorated with garlands that had seen better days, but it was cheerful. You could feel the old girl hanging on. As soon as SOAR was done with her, they'd decommission the old *Peleliu*.

And then what?

Decommission him?

He could always shift over to a Wasp-class ship. But it wouldn't be the same. He'd lived aboard this ship since his teens and it was hard to imagine being anywhere else.

He didn't like change. It was—

His eye passed over something different. Something very different. Didn't even take him a heartbeat to zero in on it.

Chief Gail Miller stood in the doorway dressed in a shining white chef's coat. Her dark red hair now shone in contrast.

He rose to meet her as she angled into the room; caught up to her as she arrived at…LCDR Ramis' table.

There was an awkward moment; he should have looked where she was going and stayed out of the way.

Sly wanted to say something about the meal. Maybe get her talking.

Ramis was in the middle of some conversation with a pair of his senior staff and looked up at her.

"You wanted to see me, sir?" Gail launched right in.

Sly was about to back off when she finally spotted him, "Hi, Chief."

She looked exhausted. Right, she'd been looking for rack time before the debrief and the meal. She must be wiped out.

Boyd turned to his table mates, "If you gentlemen would excuse us?"

They rose easily, taking their finished lunch trays back to the window.

Sly was one the verge of moving off when Ramis said, "Hang on, Chief."

Ramis waved them both to join him.

Sly ended up side by side with Gail, facing the Lieutenant Commander. Close enough that he could feel her warmth. Could smell an odd mix of cooked spices and fresh air. A smell of delicious female served up in a fine package. Her profile was well worth appreciating. Straight back evident despite the white chef's coat. Well-defined chin without being angular. Full lips and a neat nose. And—

Crap! He was doing it again. He focused his attention on the Lieutenant Commander and told it to stay there.

"That was a fine meal, Chief," Ramis started in.

It had been. Sly might be one of the few who knew why. Instead of a double grease-burger, he'd taken only one of the oversized patties and found it delicious, and enough. The guys who still took two at his table had trouble finishing them, but did anyway because they tasted so good.

"Thank you, sir. Best I could do on short notice."

"I understand you had some words with Chief Schmidt."

She glanced at Sly and he nodded that it was the same guy.

"I threw his behind in the brig, sir."

Sly was hard pressed not to laugh. *Behind.* Only a woman from the South could be in the Navy long enough to make Chief and still not put someone's *ass* in the brig.

"He's quite unhappy about the situation. I'd like to hear your side of it."

"No, sir. You wouldn't."

Ramis looked at Sly for a moment and then back at the Chief, "I assure you that I would."

Gail glanced around the room. Sly followed her gaze. Most of the officers and senior enlisted were gone. They could speak privately.

"How long have you been eating Schmidt's food, sir?"

Ramis shrugged, "Since I've been aboard, six years. Chief?"

"He came aboard two years before you did, sir."

"You *really* don't want to know. Especially not right after eating."

"I don't enjoy games, Chief."

"I don't play them, Commander."

"Except golf," Sly offered trying to lighten the moment. The poor woman had been aboard less than a single watch, and half that had been spent invading the Ivory Coast.

"Never picked up a club in my life, Chief," her smile was brief but radiant.

Twenty dollars a hole... All Sly could manage was a sputter.

"Sir," Gail switched back to being completely serious as she returned her attention to Ramis.

Didn't play golf? And he'd completely fallen for it.

Damn!

The woman found everything funny.

Except food.

He'd safely bet his pension that food was one thing she treated with a deadly seriousness.

"When I arrived in the kitchen, your chef," she managed deep disdain in the word—ocean deep, "was on the verge of seasoning your chowder with cigarette ash. He was precooking meat over thirty minutes before a meal. The coleslaw was already dressed with mayonnaise, but was not being kept at a safe temperature. His fryer oil was so dark and so far under temperature that I don't dare make French fries until I can drain and scrub the thing, that's why the potatoes were pan-fried. His vegetarian option was a bag of iceberg lettuce. Would you like me to begin discussing the state of your ship's stores or do I have permission to toss most of it overboard and order up a resupply ship?"

Ramis looked thoughtful. "Was it strictly necessary to arrest him?"

"It was the fastest way I could think of to get him out of the kitchen. It was either that or run him through the meat grinder. The galley is an interior compartment and offers no hatchways for immediate disposal at sea."

Sly couldn't help laughing. He definitely liked this woman despite his initial take on her...and her golf game.

"Your assessment, Chief Stowell?"

That sobered him, "Well, sir. I've served a lot of years with Chief Schmidt and I'm reluctant to speak ill of a fellow Chief."

He could feel Gail tensing up beside him. Woman wore her emotions right on her sleeve. How did that even happen after a decade in the Service? It was a surprise, a relief, and a wonder.

Like discovering a Christmas present had just landed on the bench beside him.

"However," Sly decided that loyalty was one thing but honesty among Chiefs was another. "It was perhaps, shall I say, ill-advised for Chief Schmidt to call Chief Miller a 'bitch' within thirty seconds of their first meeting." What the hell, in for a penny, in for a pound. "Her quick decision did have the advantage of allowing insufficient time for his barely-in-check tendencies toward sexual harassment to surface. Though his well-known disdain of all women in uniform was on full display."

"On my ship?" Ramis sounded deeply shocked.

Sly nodded confirmation. He wasn't surprised by Ramis' reaction. The man liked to delegate, through trust in his personnel, down through the ranks and didn't like to interfere on "lower" matters unless strictly needed. Missing problems like Chief Schmidt was one of the hazards of that style of command.

The Lieutenant Commander chewed on that for a moment.

Gail opened her mouth, but Sly nudged her with his knee to keep still. He could see her resist the urge to glance sideways at him, though he was fairly sure that Ramis missed it.

"Perhaps," Ramis made a show of picking up the freshly baked chocolate chip cookie that had remained on his tray throughout the discussion. "Perhaps we can return to the topic of what you put in that fine polenta dish. I'm a fair cook myself and my XO was quite insistent that I try it. I admit to being very pleasantly surprised."

# # #

"What was that?" Gail had no idea what had just happened. She gathered that she wasn't in trouble, but even that was a guess.

Sly led her down a sloping ramp and onto the Hangar Deck. It was empty except for a helicopter parked in a forward bay which was being worked on by a three-person crew. They wandered back through the cavernous space until they reached the fantail.

It was so peaceful, she could even hear their footsteps echo off the underside of the Flight Deck three stories above.

He seemed to be sticking close by her side today, not that she was complaining. When she'd been sure that he'd throw her under the keel, he'd told the truth about his long-time fellow Chief. Damned decent and totally unexpected.

Night still reigned off the stern of the ship. They were making way, but only enough to leave a minor wake. From here the stars shone brightly above. A helicopter slowly wound to life on the deck above them, only partly muted by the steel in-between.

Sly tipped his head back behind them, a movement revealed by only the faintest of light filtering down the deck from the helicopter maintenance at the far end of the bay.

"That, is Boyd Ramis' way of saying that the matter is dealt with. I think he watched too much *Upstairs, Downstairs* as a child. He's from Poughkeepsie, New York but he keeps thinking he's an understated Brit."

"So what happens to Schmidt?"

"What does and what should are two different things."

"Are you trying to be as cryptic as he is? Give me a break, Sly, and spell it out." The helicopter, now at full roar, lifted off the Flight Deck and made a quick turn for the west, disappearing into the darkness.

"See that helo?"

"Sure." Its winking lights were rapidly disappearing from sight.

"I'd wager that Chief Vic Schmidt is aboard, heading over to the carrier to catch a ride home. Ramis might seem obtuse or lax, but he is also a man who believes in immediate action and he doesn't tolerate problems…once he learns of them."

Gail could hear the bad with the good in Sly's tone, but overall she was encouraged. She'd served with commanders who were far less appreciated by their crews, and deservedly so.

"Vic was due to muster out after handing over the galley to you. Everyone expected that to take two weeks, not two minutes," he offered a shrug. "He'll get his Honorable Discharge, maybe even a rank bump for time served to bolster his pension, and live to tell stories about the 'bitch' who replaced him."

"Jerk."

Sly laughed.

"What?"

"Even now you can't curse him? What kind of a girl are you?"

"*I'm a good girl, I am.*" She made it sound as if she was quoting something in a poor Cockney accent with a little bit of South still slipping through.

He didn't even get the joke and still she made him want to laugh. When was the last time a woman made him feel that way? Never? Twice never? He brushed her hair back behind her ear so that he could see her profile more clearly.

She didn't flinch or pull away despite how forward the action was.

"I," his throat had gone dry, "I think that I am the one about to be a jerk."

She turned to look at him. Really look at him.

Even in the shadowed darkness of the distant worklights he could feel her studying him intently.

"I suspect that being a jerk isn't the real you, Chief."

"Let's find out." Then Sly did something he'd never done before in two decades of service, he kissed a woman while on a Naval vessel.

# # #

Gail was not a loose woman.

Telling herself that didn't sound very convincing at the moment. What had started as a testing kiss had heated right up when she leaned into it.

She'd known the man for maybe fifteen seconds and here she was throwing herself at him.

Sly slid his arms around her and pulled her in.

She let him.

He wasn't just Navy strong; he worked at it. She could feel the strength of him, both physical and…she didn't even have the right word. But from somewhere down inside him there was a core of seriously good, like the rich center of a wrapped filet mignon…except he struck her as more of a corndog kind of guy—an analogy that also worked. Sort of.

It didn't stop her from enjoying the kiss that he was giving her. That she was giving back.

Loose woman.

Well, maybe just this once it was okay.

There'd been something about him from that first moment standing there with his pants and his dignity all wet.

She managed to step back by a half breath, but it was a struggle when her body was screaming to go in the other direction.

"Holy cats, Chief!" she struggled for control of her racing heart, but that attempt went right out the porthole along with not being "loose."

"Holy cats?"

"Do you greet all new Chiefs this way?" He still held her tight against him and she could see no reason to try and escape. He felt wonderful.

"Not as a habit, no."

She closed her eyes for a moment and went looking around inside for a bit of sanity, but that appeared to be out of stock in the Gail Miller pantry.

"For one thing, the guys never shave close enough and are always scratchy."

She ran a hand over his face.

"Some of the women too."

Very smooth. Too smooth.

"You shave especially for me, Chief?"

"Didn't think I was went I did it, but I might have been."

"Hmm…" Gail never just purred like a cat, but she certainly felt like one at the moment. Canary and all.

He waited her out, his strong hands had slid from her back down to her waist when she moved back, but he hadn't pulled away. He was a man confident in his own attraction.

"I wish…" she trailed off.

"What?"

She brushed that smooth cheek again and looked up into those dark, waiting eyes. "That I had more than the three minutes I need to get back to my galley. The crew will be there by then."

Sly stepped back. "Well, perhaps later, Chief."

"No perhaps about it, Chief. That's a 'definitely.' If that kiss was any indicator, you're well worth the risk of a court martial."

Then she turned and headed away fast.

It was either that or throw herself at him, knock them both off the stern railing, and die happy in the warm ocean.

Definitely a loose woman.

Which did leave her to wonder quite where she'd left the old Gail Miller when she was stowing her gear for the trip to the *Peleliu.*

Chapter 7

It took five days of exhausting work to turn around the galley to the point where she didn't want to cringe each time she walked into it.

Gail had recruited any able-bodied seaman who wasn't fast enough to duck and cover. Mechanics had replaced leaky lines and questionable power outlets. The overhead piping and hoods had been scraped of old grease, scrubbed, and repainted—plenty of gray paint aboard. The galley was spit-shine bright by the time they were done with it.

The ship's stores weren't as miserable as she'd first thought, they'd simply been pillaged at random and not restowed properly. A long day in the tropics wearing Arctic survival gear put everything to rights.

A vast jumble of produce had turned into a sensible set of supplies once organized. The meat locker—almost void of ground chuck, clearly the former chef's perennial go-to meal—flowed with roasts and chops and all the finer cuts that the chef had disdained as being "too much trouble." The dairy, other than where the chef had clearly dropped a case of eggs then kicked them under a shelf, came through in good shape as well.

When Gail had scrubbed her kitchen, she'd also scrubbed his name from her mind. She granted him "chef" in her thoughts, a title he definitely didn't deserve, simply to save herself from far more foul references.

The staff were another matter. Her master baker and butcher were good, it simply took them a while to come to their senses and realize they had the freedom to do decent work.

The main trait of her galley staff was that they were young, overeager, and undertrained. The "chef" had chased away anyone who cared about food except for the few who were too green to know better—or get a transfer out.

Third Class Petty Officer Jimmy Roltz, a thin black kid from Oklahoma with the unexpected nickname of "Tanker," had been within days of his transfer coming through. Once she saw how good he was, she'd talked him out of it and made him her sous chef.

For a couple days she held them to the one-hour break between meals, until they dug out the galley. The first day she gave them a two-hour break, she stayed on alone, finally able to plan a menu rather than simply react to the clock with whatever she could lay her hands on.

After an hour, Tanker drifted in, glanced over her shoulder, and moved over to fire up one of the big griddles. By fifteen minutes later the whole crew was back. Frying bacon filtered into the air from Tanker's cook top.

Gail did her best to keep her composure, but she wanted to go around and hug every one of them.

Someone put on Christmas music, an a cappella group she didn't know. They were good. She'd have to tell Mama.

Tanker began working up a carbonara sauce in between tending the bacon.

"Who here knows how to make fresh pasta?"

Tanker was the only one.

"Tanker, no pepper in your sauce. I've got an idea. Okay everyone, gather around."

Teaching was her favorite part of cooking. The only daughter of two university professors, was it any wonder.

# # #

"Oh my god!" Sly closed his eyes to appreciate the mouthful he'd just taken.

The flavors unfolded on him, cream, garlic, and bacon with an underlying accent of pepper. Wine, parmesan…the layers just kept appearing.

"What's with the pasta?" Dave was poking it with his fork like it was going to jump out of the bowl and attack him.

Sly savored it just a moment longer as Tom answered him.

"That's fresh spaghetti, you goon."

"Fettuccini," Sly corrected him.

"Fresh? Like fresh-made. How do you even make *fet-tu-chi-ni?*" he harassed Sly. "And why's it all speckly?"

"It's fresh-made pepper pasta and the way you make it this good, I'll be damned if I know."

"Hey, Sly," Tom pointed at his own bowl of pasta. "You gotta try this."

Dave looked over, "Why's it all green? That can't be right."

"It's made with vegetables and shit," Tom told him.

Sly dug out a forkful of bright green spinach pasta and made a point of stabbing up a tomato and a Kalamata olive while he was at it. Garlic and olive exploded across his palate.

"Damn, you could power our boat on this stuff it's so good."

Sly scanned the mess. Navy swabbies liked their chow, but there was something different going on here—it was rippling across the crowded mess. People were trying each other's meals, actually talking about their food instead of the latest assignment or the latest babe. A lot of sailors going back for seconds. There'd been consistently better food in the five days since Gail Miller showed up, but this was incredible. Something had happened in the kitchen and he had no idea what.

Which was making him more than a little crazy.

She'd kissed him like…he didn't know what. Like a woman didn't kiss a man she'd just met. Especially not one who had just claimed she was *a good girl she was*. And then she'd evaporated like a keg of beer at a barbeque, there and then gone.

He'd gone looking for her a couple times—more than a couple if the truth be told.

One time he'd caught up with her in the galley, and spent two hours scrubbing the outsides of the steam kettles.

He tried the galley again, after the heavy work was done—which had included he, Dave and Tom emptying a walk-in cooler and resealing all of the galvanized sheet metal seams—except that time she'd gone aft and down to ship's stores. When he'd arrived down there, it was to learn that she'd gone to the baker to port, the butcher to starboard, the potato peeling room amidships, and then forward and back up two decks to the galley once more.

Woman was a whirlwind.

Word was she was even working with the midrats crew in the middle of her sleep shift to make sure the Navy off-watch crew was well taken care off.

Well, she wasn't getting away with it this time. Being in the Navy had taught him patience, but there had to be some limits.

He took his tray back the moment he was done, resisted grabbing another piece of fresh-baked garlic bread, with the garlic roasted first until it was so sweet it tasted like honey for crying out loud, and went for a piece of apple pie that was—he took a forkful—still warm from being baked. Not just some frozen thing thawed under a heat lamp, *Damn!* He ate on the move as he headed for the galley before the service ended.

His arrival was perfectly timed for the end of his pie and the end of the meal service.

Gail was still moving full tilt about the kitchen, but the difference from five days ago was that her crew was moving just as fast. There was an energy here, an excitement that he hadn't seen around the *Peleliu* galley in a long time.

He stood in the doorway and watched.

They were talking about tomorrow's service and chasing around ideas.

He waited them out.

It wasn't a short wait. They were twenty minutes off shift before the group broke up.

As it did, he moved quickly, dropping his plate and fork in the scullery sink on his way. It was already immaculate from the meal service cleanup. A pretty little Asian Seaman scowled at him, as if he was being a heathen, and paused long enough to rinse and load his offending dinnerware into an otherwise empty dishwasher tray before she hung her apron and departed.

Chief Steward Gail Miller sat at the shining expanse of the stainless steel prep table that filled the center of the galley. The down-lights made her shine—her bright face, her immaculate white coat. She looked as marvelous as her food.

He leaned on the side opposite her as she concentrated on some list.

Sly could watch her for hours.

Her long fingers were neat and her writing fast. A shopping list, ingredients for tomorrow's meals by the date across the top. The part in her hair tempted him to reach out and run a finger down it.

He resisted.

Her hair hung down to either side of her face.

"Good evening, Chief."

# # #

Gail looked at her watch—five a.m. Oh, right. It was evening by the *Peleliu's* operational cycle. She still didn't have the hang of that.

Then she looked up at Chief Stowell leaning on the table as if he'd been there a while. Watching her.

"Evening," she managed. Not seeing Sly for five days—except when she'd been begging him for help and about a hundred times out of the corner of her eye—always gone when she turned to really look—she'd managed forget how perfect he looked.

Blisteringly handsome? No. Too many men boasted that and it was often their only good attribute. But Sly was awfully good-looking.

Strong. Tonight he wore khakis and a Navy blue t-shirt that clung to his upper body. She'd been able to feel his strength when they'd kissed. Couldn't seem to stop thinking about that actually. But to see it on display was breathtaking. Again, not bodybuilder, just powerful.

If myths were to be believed, he'd personally bested all of the Rangers aboard in a wrestling match. And some of those guys made Sly look small.

Word was he'd even taken on the head Delta operator; that was too much of stretch.

But looking at him, she could almost believe it.

He looked exactly like he was, a totally stand-up guy. He drove one of the Navy's strangest transports with a mixture of grace and panache. Her staff lived in the galley, yet they still mentioned him from time to time and always with a tone of respect.

Gail had spent five days trying to pigeonhole Sly Stowell in her head, with little luck. Her attempts to brush off their one kiss as an aberration were equally successful—as in not at all.

She wasn't used to stand-up guys. Other chefs, well, they worked hard and drank hard. Even the Navy ones, who mostly kept their drunkenness ashore because ships were dry. But there were a lot of hung-over culinary specialists working the line at the landside bases. And the civilian restaurant world made the Navy sots look sober and clean by comparison.

"Do you drink beer?" Just how straight was this man leaning against the far side of her steel worktable?

"You offering?" his smile noted how unusual that would be aboard ship.

"Asking." Nitpicker.

"On occasion."

"When?" Why was she even asking? Why was she even interested?

"Depends."

"On what?" *On how exasperating he could be?*

"On what the meal is. Barbeque is always beer food. That dinner you made tonight, that wants a wine—a good one. And I'm not a wine sort of guy."

"I'll assume that's a compliment."

"No," he dragged it out just to tick her off, so she refused to buy in. "Compliment is too simple a word for that meal. Been aboard nineteen years and haven't had a whole lot of dinners that tasted as good as that one."

"Nineteen years? I was in high school, a freshman."

"I went in on the day I graduated."

"I enlisted a month out of college."

"Why?"

Gail clambered to her feet and popped open one of the fridges. The prior "chef" had left behind a large collection of pint-sized bottles of orange juice. She'd wager that was to hide the vodka in his screwdriver; time to work her way through his juice stash, she hadn't found the alcohol stash yet, hoped she never did. She offered a juice to Sly, who nodded, and she came back with two.

She sat back down and kicked a stool out from under the counter, and apparently caught him sharply on the shin.

"Oops! Sorry. That was supposed to be a friendly gesture."

"Right, thanks," he settled on the stool and toasted her with his now open juice.

She returned the gesture, "Mama and Daddy teach at The Citadel. Made military seem like a natural choice after I went to the Art Institute's culinary program." Which was about a quarter of the truth. The rest? That was for her alone.

"Charleston, thought so."

Man was too sure of himself. His accent was harder to place, it was mostly Navy.

Something about the way he'd said *barbeque.*

"Oh no. Lexington, North Carolina."

"Got a good ear there, Chief."

"Got two of them, Chief. Just like I've got two eyes. Healthy human female. And don't you dare mention what else I have two of. But that's not real barbeque that you cook up north. That's pork in tomato sauce. You're killing the poor pig. Twice! What did it do to deserve that?"

His grin was wicked and ready for battle, "Mustard, vinegar, chicken bouillon? You gotta be kidding me. We're in the South, not Germany for crying out loud."

"Actually, we're off the Ivory Coast, Africa, Chief."

"No, we're headed west. Don't know where, no one is talking to me yet. We're not in a big hurry or you'd hear the engines even in here. Maybe we're just going to visit the local carrier group."

Gail considered, but it didn't affect her. Still, carrier group. They'd probably have a resupply ship along. Some fresh produce and real spices would be a good thing. And she probably should get some more ground chuck.

"You're changing the topic, Chief," she accused him. "Trying to distract me with the lame excuse of some hometown barbeque you've eaten."

"Not just eaten. Cooked. And yeah, I'm trying to distract you, but not from that."

Gail eyed him more carefully. "Cooked? On your backyard barbie?"

"Cooked!" he made it a challenge. "I worked my first festival tent when I was ten years old."

She had to admit that the Lexington Barbeque Festival was notorious. She might have made it there a time or two herself, not that she'd be admitting it anytime soon.

"I've only missed two years since. Last year we did over twenty thousand pounds out of three festival tents." He thumped a fist on the table. "*That* is god damn barbeque."

The real joke here was he might well have served her a pulled pork sandwich in some year past. He was so cute about defending his home turf that she couldn't help herself. She leaned across the table, managed to snag his collar, and pulled him in.

His kiss tasted of her carbonara sauce and apple pie.

She let it grow and build there in the middle of her kitchen until she wondered that the fire suppression system didn't kick on. Thinking about having kissed Chief Stowell once and kissing him again now were a whole world apart.

"You gotta get me somewhere better than this kitchen, Chief," she mumbled it against his lips.

"Uh—"

If he put her off or hedged, she was going dump her orange juice on his head. After a kiss like that, he'd better not be playing around. That wasn't just some kiss, that one was a game changer.

"I know just the place." He brushed his lips over hers and went to drag her out of the galley.

She barely managed to douse the lights as she followed.

# # #

"Here?" Gail looked at him.

"Been thinking about you here, since—" Sly tried desperately to get control of his libido, but that didn't work so well, his mental gauges were running at overload. The woman kissed like a wonder and tasted like a crime just waiting to happen. "Since the first time you came aboard."

"You mean since the first time you decided I wasn't an idiot bimbo. 'Oh, what a beautiful Christmas tree!'" she mimicked herself in a ridiculous tone. Did a good job of it too as her voice echoed off the sides of the Well Deck.

"Okay," he slid that sideways smile into place. "After that."

The Well Deck was lit by only a few dim worklights. The rear gate was up and sealed, the wood-plank deck itself was dry. It was still night in the gap above the top of the gate. His LCAC rested at the foot of the garage slope with both front and rear ramps folded down.

Finally out of the public spaces, he took her hand once more. The shock was electric and he could tell that she felt it as well.

"Too fast," he knew it was true the moment he said it.

And hated himself. Sly never took things fast, but he wanted to with Gail Miller. He wanted to tease her until that laugh burst forth and showered over the both of them.

"I'm sorry. It's too fast. I shouldn't—"

She kissed him. Not hot and heavy like in the galley. Just enough to stop his words rather than his heart.

"Let's walk," she kept a hold of his hand. "Let's just go for a walk."

And they did. They walked the hundred meters of the Well Deck as if it were a pier at the Norfolk Navy Yard. They walked together in slow silence until he could see that the starlight showing above the top of the rear gate had started to fade.

She was the first to break the quiet, asking him about his early days on the *Peleliu*.

He in turn asked her how in the hell she'd made that amazing pasta.

As they strolled back and forth over the heavy wooden planking, the stars faded and the sky shifted from black to darkest blue in the gap above the rear gate.

It was going orange when she led him aboard the LCAC and up to the control room. There she turned on the tiny Christmas tree and they undressed each other by its light.

He got over the embarrassment of having brought protection quickly enough. He sat in the observer's chair and she straddled over him.

Sly had many fine moments in his life worth remembering. He'd delivered thousands of Marines over the years, rescued hundreds, maybe thousands more of near-panicked civilians from hostile shores. He'd held many fine women kind enough to share their body with him.

Never had he held a woman like the one who made silent love by the light of a foot-tall Christmas tree.

Where he'd expected laughter, he elicited soft moans. Instead of the deep wildness that burst forth in her kisses, she was like one of her sauces—so smooth and perfect that he could spend ages investigating and tasting. Creamy skin. Rich flavors. Strong reactions that left a man hungry for more no matter how much he took.

Still facing him, she leaned back in his arms until her elbows rested on the backs of his and Tom's control chairs. He leaned down to drink her in, to feast upon her. He felt like a child before her and, in the same moment, like a powerful man welcomed to a lover's arms.

For all the frantic need that had built up over the last five days, a need he'd only barely been aware of, they were very gentle with one another. Cresting over the slow-arriving waves with a sigh rather than a gasp.

He knew the rest was there. The wildness, the desire to give and take on a grand scale. But for this one moment he was shocked into gentleness by the discovery of her.

Gail Miller. A wonder of a woman.

When their heart rate had returned from the stratosphere, a thin lance of the rising sun shone in over the Well Deck rear gate and outshone the light of the little tree. Sly knew his world had indeed shifted.

It was wrong in so many ways, but he wanted all he could get of this woman. Once would never be enough, no matter how perfect the meal.

She brushed her lips lightly over his and then held him close and whispered in his ear.

"Chief?"

"Yeah?" he managed.

"That stuff you do?"

"Uh-huh?" He nuzzled her neck again and elicited the sigh of contentment he had discovered there. He wondered just how fast he'd be ready to do more of that "stuff" he did. Sly already knew that the next time they were together would be as wild as this time had been sublime.

"That still isn't barbeque."

It was rude to laugh in the face of a naked woman still straddled across your lap, but that's exactly what he did.

Chapter 8

M*atheo!*"

"*Ma bien-aimée!*" Matheo Chastain practically shouted over the ship-to-ship comm circuit.

The call had been routed to Gail's cabin. She was barely awake.

"How is your life being, my love?"

"Good," Gail insisted. After what she and Sly had done to each other's bodies last night—this morning, whatever it was—it was very hard to complain. It was, she checked her watch, an hour until it was time to start prep on this evening's breakfast service.

She finally felt she had some form of control on the *Peleliu's* galley and mess. Another triumph. Now she was ready to begin with some of her long-term plans.

And Sly Stowell. While she didn't have plans there, she was definitely looking forward to a rematch. Their second time, he'd laid her back against the rear of the LCAC's control cabin and blown rationality right out of her brain. They'd driven at each other until they both dripped with sweat. It was a good thing the windows had been replaced or their cries would have echoed about the Well Deck. She shifted in her bunk and felt deliciously achy.

She was doing, "Very good."

"*Very good?* That is not what I am hearing," Matheo's voice regrounded her in the moment. "But when I consider the source, perhaps it is high praise indeed."

"What source?"

Matheo's parents had moved from a small town outside of Riems, France to just down the street from Gail's childhood home in South Carolina. He was in junior high school and Gail was just starting to wonder what kindergarten might be like. He had made his English American-perfect by graduation, and then totally regressed by the time he was her culinary instructor at the Art Institute of Charleston. It was at least partly her fault he'd gone on to be a Navy chef; she'd coaxed him into signing up together. He must like it though, as he'd stayed in.

"The source, it was a totally despicable man who was allowed in my galley for mere minutes. My guest at the time was the group admiral, so they were minutes poorly spent by *Monsieur* Schmidt. He is lucky he did not leave my galley in irons. He is now a Second Class Petty Officer though I fear little humbled. He behaves only because he wishes his discharge to remain honorable. The admiral, he threatened to make this man swim home."

"Well, I actually did have him tossed in the brig, though I don't know if it ended up on his record."

"*Parfait!* You must come see me and tell me about it."

She laughed, "That could be a while. Wait. You saw Schmidt? Where are you anyway?" Maybe he'd seen him during the man's transit back to stateside.

"I am aboard the *George H. W. Bush,* sweetheart."

"Wow!" The newest aircraft carrier in the fleet. That was *the* premier mess in the Navy. There were bigger messes ashore, but the prestige rested with this newest carrier.

"You must come see. I want to show it to you, my Gail. I must ask you things."

"I'm in Africa right now Matheo."

"Yes."

"What?" she'd missed something.

"You are in Africa. I am also."

"Africa's a big place, Matheo. You were never good with time and distance." Such things were unendingly elusive to the man, but he was a masterful chef.

"Yes, but whether I am a thousand meters off your port bow or two thousand I think is making little difference."

# # #

The sun was rising once more by the time Gail arrived at the *Bush*. She hadn't even had time to discover which ship she'd landed on in her transit to the *Peleliu* they'd moved her along so fast.

Looking up from the small Zodiac boat that Sly had used to deliver her, she was monstrous. The CVN-76 displaced a hundred thousand tons to *Peleliu's* forty. Her six-thousand person crew would need two *Pelelius* and they still wouldn't fit aboard. And instead of carrying a mere eight highly specialized helicopters, though she could load on twenty if needed, the *George H.W. Bush* carried nearly a hundred jet fighters and heavy-lift helos.

Sly pulled them up to the floating dock that hung down her side and tied off. The sea was calm enough for them to leave the boat here and climb the stairs up to the mid-level hatch.

"I needed a couple of parts from their chief mechanic anyway," Sly had said when he offered to motor her across.

In sharp contrast to the *Peleliu* that appeared to wander the world's oceans on her own, the *Bush* claimed a carrier group for company: a guided missile cruiser, two warships, a pair of destroyers, and miscellaneous oilers and tenders for company. The ocean felt very crowded around the massive ship.

Jets roared aloft and into the blue sky with painful regularity, forcing her to cover her ears time and again during the ascent of the stairs. A look back showed the *Peleliu's* deck to be quiet and the helos shrouded once more. She'd heard them out on exercises during the various night-time meal services, but it was daylight now and they were done.

At the head of the stairs a Seaman First Class awaited her.

"I'll come find you after," she offered Sly and then realized that was a stupid thing to say. If she'd get lost on the *Peleliu* then she didn't stand a chance here.

The man simply grinned at her.

"Perhaps you better come and find me in an hour or so. I'll be close by the galley."

He saluted, "Yes, ma'am, Chief."

She saluted back and matched him grin for grin, "As you were, Chief."

# # #

The galley aboard the aircraft carrier was much bigger than hers and thirty years newer. Suddenly the mileage and the years on the *Peleliu* showed.

Gail had been so proud of her new command, but her galley was half the size. The battering of hard service that couldn't be removed by hard scrubbing and fresh paint didn't appear here. Instead of a dozen willing hands, plus two more on the midrats shift, here there were a dozen working the line. More tended steam kettles, oven, mixers, blenders…

Breakfast service was at full roar. Mile-long griddles were buried in pancakes. Gallon pitchers of maple syrup were pulled from the warmers. Waffles, eggs, link sausage—it was a mass of food that would feed her six hundred charges for days.

And this was only the main galley. How many did a carrier have?

"Sweetheart!"

And she was lost in Matheo's bear hug. He held her close and hard. Enough for her to remember what it had been like to be his lover. It had started the day she graduated culinary school and was no longer his student. For a month they had rarely left his bed. Over the years since, when they were both between lovers, they would plan leave together in some corner or other of the world that was convenient or had a regional cuisine neither of them had tasted before. The last time had been three years ago in southern Thailand. A sun-soaked holiday she remembered well.

But now—she pulled back—she was not between lovers. She and Sly had spent only a single night together—not even that—but it had been one that definitely counted.

"Ah," Matheo felt the shift and acknowledged it sadly with a great sigh she could feel ripple along his chest. "My timing is not so lucky. Is it serious?"

"Too soon to tell." They had always confided in each other, picked each other up afterward, patched bruised egos, and sent one another on their way with a kiss, or more if they were unattached at the time.

"Then there is still hope for me," he moved back but kept an arm around her shoulder and they both turned to face the galley once more. "Is it not an amazing sight, my sweet?"

"It is, Matheo. And she's yours?"

"Yes, all seven galleys."

Seven? She had one galley and two messes. Seven was…just like the ship…monstrous.

"Come let us have breakfast together."

"I just finished dinner."

He looked at her strangely and she wondered how much she was even allowed to say.

"We're on an odd training schedule at the moment."

That appeared to satisfy him.

She took a cup of coffee and kept him company while he whipped up a quick omelette. Gail had many fond memories of his omelettes. Smoked salmon in bed had been her first introduction to it outside the classroom. A red curry with Kung haeng shrimp cooked in a grass hut on a Thai beach had been the last; again served in bed.

She tasted a corner of his when he offered a forkful. It was so simple that the perfection of it showed through as the key element.

"Chive and fresh basil," she sighed. She was awfully glad that the aircraft carriers were in a different class of the Admiral Ney Food Service Awards than her ship or she wouldn't stand a chance.

In the competition, there were the aircraft carriers, then the "large afloat" category which included the *Peleliu* even with her reduced crew. Below that were "medium," "small," and "submarine." There were ten ships in both the "aircraft carrier" and "large afloat" categories. That at least was fair between them. She'd desperately like to out-cook Matheo, though there was little chance of ever doing that.

He led her to a small office off the side of the galley, plate in one hand, coffee in the other. The full-throated roar of the beast—chopping thunks, dishwasher, calls up and down the lines for refills of pans that rang loud with their emptiness—was muted but far from gone. It was a world they both lived and loved. To shut it out would not be a comfort to either of them.

She had so much in common with Matheo.

That gave Gail a pause. They did have so much in common. What did she and Sly have?

A heat, that she suspected they had only begun to discover. Both being the same rank, well, they were both Chiefs, the same first word of their rank—the Stewards department was its own thing. And they each despised the others' taste in barbeque, on grounds of principle if not for reasons of the palate. Not much else.

"So, *chérie*, I must speak quickly so that you may return to your little boat in time for lunch service." He ate his omelette in slow leisurely bites. Even when in a hurry, Matheo had always slowed down to appreciate anything he was eating.

She didn't correct him on that assumption. The midrats crew would have the rest of the "day" well in hand. It was coming up on her own bedtime.

"I wish we had the time to show you all of my ship."

Gail knew full well what else he would like to show her and normally she'd be as eager as he was. Not this time. Not even a little. His amorous attentions weren't even raising her pulse rate which was curious; he was always able to do that no matter who she was with. An incredibly handsome chef with a dashing French accent who was also a very dear friend—normally an intoxicating combination.

"Instead, I must be very American and blunt. I want you, *chérie!*"

"You what?" Gail wondered where that had come from. Matheo always respected her relationships with others as she did his. And she'd just said she was in one.

"Well, I would like you for that as well, my dear Gail. But I need you. Here!" he pointed a forkful of omelette emphatically toward the door and almost lost the bite. "You belong *here!*"

He couldn't mean—

"Seven galleys. Six thousand people I must feed. Eighteen thousand meals a day, I feed a small city. It is *insensé!* You must leave your little ship and come help me. We will cook like we once did, together. And who knows, maybe you cook with me, you forget about..." he offered her a very Gallic shrug.

He was watching her carefully.

"...or perhaps not."

How had he read that in her face? *She* didn't even know how she felt about Sly yet. Goodness, she didn't even know if that was a nickname or a birth name.

"Either way, my Gail. You must think. I need a sous chef *désespérément.* Consider. You and me. As you said so long ago in my little Charleston apartment. The Admiral Ney Award for the largest boat in the world. Wouldn't that be something worth doing together? You tell me what must I do to have you and it will happen. Anything. *Oui?*"

"*Oui*," she managed weakly. "I'll think on it."

# # #

Gail was very quiet on the ride back to the *Peleliu*.

Sly didn't like that. Something was wrong.

Nor had he liked the way the Chief Steward aboard the *Bush* had hugged her goodbye. No salute or handshake. Instead he had hugged her tightly and she had rested her head on his shoulder.

He wouldn't ask.

It was her business.

But damn it! Wasn't it his as well?

He just couldn't figure out how to start that conversation. So, they rode in silence back to their boat, picked up the falls from the davits, and latched them to the Zodiac boat fore and aft. The winch lifted them aloft by those lines until the boat was tucked back in its cubbyhole high on the outside of the hull, close beneath the Flight Deck.

Sly offered a hand to help her out of the boat, just for an excuse to touch her. To confirm that he wasn't totally shut out.

She looked at the offered hand for a long moment.

"Where's your part?"

"What part?"

She watched him a moment and then smiled sadly.

Part? Right! Crap! He'd said he'd take her to the carrier because he wanted to fetch a part from their chief mechanic. Instead he'd sat in the ready room lounge sipping a cherry Coke and watched one set of planes land and another set take off.

One look at her face told him it was too late to backpedal now, so he offered a shrug. *You caught me.* Was it so wrong to be nice to his...well, he went looking for another word, but "lover" was the only one he came up with.

She took his hand and squeezed it tightly, far more tightly than she needed to maintain her balance out of the boat and into the hatchway.

He used his hand to stop her, until she turned to face him.

He thought about asking if this was about them, but how did you ask that of someone you barely knew and had made love to just last night. That glorious moment that he couldn't wait to repeat. So, he changed his question.

"Gail," it felt a little odd calling her by name rather than Chief. Odd but good. "If you need to talk about anything, I hope you'll think to talk to me."

In the privacy of the little alcove, five decks above the sea, she patted him on the chest.

"You'll be the first, Sly. Thanks."

Then she did the strangest thing, considering the circumstances. She went up on her toes and kissed him lightly before proceeding inside.

Sly took his time battening down the boat and pulling the cover back in place as he watched the big aircraft carrier in the distance, riding on the shining sea.

Chapter 9

Gail wished she'd slept.

She wished she'd made love to Sly. Right there. In the little boat, in the privacy of the little cubbyhole high on the *Peleliu's* side, exposed only to the sea. Let him purge the doubt from her. For she was filled with doubt in all its many flavors.

So, she did the only thing she knew how to do.

She cooked.

Matheo served pancakes to the crew and an omelette for himself.

She showed her staff how to make omelettes for six hundred. A massive undertaking to have just the right amount of air whipped into the eggs when they hit the pan. That crucial moment of sprinkling the sausage and cream cheese filling after the bottom was gelled but before the top began to set so that the fillings were integrated right into the eggs. Regulating the production so that they never sat on the line for more than moments, yet no one was kept waiting.

Omelettes were labor intensive, but that didn't scare her, though it nearly killed her staff. It took until mid-service before they'd settled into the nearly silent state that chefs found when everything was in perfect intense flow. When the end of service was in sight, they'd moved to the next level where they could laugh and joke with each other because there was no need to worry about the actual production of the food any longer. They needed more eggs? Someone else had already placed them in just the right spot. A fresh round of sausage? It was sizzling to finished perfection on the griddle at this very moment.

When the last omelette was served, she told the crew she needed a dozen more.

Two minutes later they were flying out of the pans.

By the time the line had them made she'd cleared a space down the center table and spread a dozen plates. She slid toasted slices of the fresh-baked whole wheat bread out of the oven and onto each plate. Three flavors of jam down the middle.

In moments, the meal was set and her staff looked confused.

"Sit," she told them simply. "About time we ate together."

Tanker reached for the ketchup and she slapped his hand.

The meal was a merry one.

# # #

With the smaller crew aboard *Peleliu* there was a lot of job overlap. Sly had always enjoyed that aspect of the shipboard life. If you wanted to stretch yourself, there were plenty of opportunities. He'd been cross-trained on dozens of aspects of operations. Over the years he'd worked gunnery control, stood watch, and was a fair hand in engineering spaces. And they all trained in fire suppression.

But ship's stores was one he wished he hadn't been trained in. A couple of the non-stealth SOAR helicopters were working back and forth between the supply ship and the *Peleliu*. They were flying so fast that the massive pallets of supplies, each wrapped in its own cargo net, were building up faster than he and his team could move them with their forklifts.

The supply ship floated only thirty meters away. A fuel hose had been run across on a wire, and diesel was pouring through it for the ship and the Rangers' few vehicles. Another line delivered Jet A for the helicopters and his LCAC.

Machinery, personnel and supplies were moving around so fast that mayhem was a far nearer state than order. At moments like this he kept waiting for someone to pick up a load and back up right off the side of the ship; and he was always afraid it was going to be him. For some idiot reason, it wasn't the fifteen meters of freefall that worried him; it was the looking stupid.

And the fear tripled the moment he spotted Gail Miller up on deck.

He zipped over to her in his forklift.

"Hi Chief. That was some fine breakfast you made."

She shaded her eyes against the setting sun to look at him. "Breakfast at sunset. I'm still not used to that."

"We switched over six months ago and I'm not either."

That earned him a smile. Better than she'd offered when they returned this morning, but still not her usual dazzler.

"Whoops!" he spotted another bird leaving the supply ship. "Must run."

"Be careful with my dry goods!"

"You promise to make more meals like that one, Chief, and I can guarantee it."

"I'm just getting started."

Sly didn't ask the next question, *Were they "over" before they'd really gotten started?*

He drove off before she'd be able to see the question on his face in the shadowy light.

# # #

Gail hadn't expected to see Sly when she'd come up on deck for some fresh air. She'd actually been thinking of getting as far away from him as possible.

His hovercraft was parked six decks below. It lay at the water level and here she stood looking up at the sunset sky.

So, of course, he was here.

And of course he had hurried over, spotting her the very second she'd stepped onto the Flight Deck. Couldn't the man be some oblivious jerk who bedded a woman and moved on, looking awkwardly aside ever after.

No.

Instead he'd proven himself considerate, funny, and had carefully driven away the moment the dark shadows of doubt crossed over his features.

She wanted to retreat back to the steel safety of her galley. Pull on the white cloak and hat of "chef" and disappear back into her own cocoon of familiarity. But that would be the coward's way—a path she could never follow once she recognized it.

Instead, she threaded a path through the stacks of un-netted pallets of supplies. One box said Library. A pile of mailbags were strapped to another. A long pair of boxes, each less than a meter high and wide, and almost a dozen long was labeled "MH-60M rotor blades" for one of the Black Hawk helicopters.

Her supplies were being stacked on the bomb elevator and were headed down to the big coolers, freezers, and storage areas on Fourth Deck. Machinery was being loaded onto the aircraft elevator for a ride down to the Hangar Deck. Each parcel would be in its place inside the hour. Or if mis-stowed, forever lost in the labyrinthine ship.

Like one Chief Steward Gail Miller.

Why in the world was she on a Special Forces ship?

It was another point in favor of accepting Matheo's offer. On something as big and complex as the *George H.W. Bush* her role would be very clearly defined. Bounded. Comprehensible.

She wanted to take an apple corer and remove the part of her brain that wouldn't stop worrying at this problem. She'd done little else since speaking with Matheo.

Finally escaping the twists, turns, and temporary alleyways of stacked supplies, she walked up the deck away from Sly and the other workers.

Just to frustrate herself, she stopped before she reached the first shrouded helicopter and looked back at the forklifts buzzing around the deck. One had a different pattern of movement than all the others.

That forklift was Sly Stowell.

She couldn't even see its color in the fading daylight, not yet fully replaced by the bright deck lighting. But there was no question which was his. He drove a forklift the way he flew an LCAC, clean. The man simply stood out from the crowd. He did it without bragging or being obnoxious.

He simply did. That was all.

She...didn't need to keep thinking about that.

Gail turned away and barely suppressed a scream when she saw the tall chief pilot of SOAR standing not two steps behind her.

"Sorry. Didn't mean to spook you. Chief Warrant Lola Maloney."

"I remember," Gail took a breath while her heart rate dropped slowly.

"Thinking deep thoughts there, Chief Miller. Thought you were going to run me right over."

"Sorry, Chief. I was simply going for a walk."

"Well, no question about you being from the South, apologizing for everything between one breath and the next. And if you promise not to Chief Warrant me, I won't Chief Steward you. Want some company?"

Gail didn't want to spill out her thoughts all over a stranger, but... "I'd love some. I really need to *stop* thinking."

Lola simply grinned at her until Gail heard her own words.

Gail opened her mouth to apologize, but Lola raised her hand to stop her.

"You gotta cut that out, girl."

"The apologizing, the thinking, or the being rude?"

"Well, the first two at a minimum." Lola said it flat.

"Think I'm going to like you, Lola."

"Jes' wait 'til y'all gets to know me," she said with a rolling Creole accent that was there one moment and gone the next. "N'awlins," she offered by way of explanation.

"Haven't been there since Mardi Gras while I was still in school. We made a field trip out of it and ate our way through the French Quarter. Before, well, before."

"Before Katrina tried to kill my city. I know."

Gail resisted the "sorry."

"So, I've got an important question."

"As long as I don't have to think." And the question had better not be about Chief Petty Officer Sly Stowell or the aircraft carrier that still floated nearby.

Lola laughed, "I know how to serve up twenty omelettes out of a kitchen; that's how many girls Mama Raci had."

"Your mama had twenty daughters?"

"Did I say they were daughters?"

"Uh," that meant…"Oh."

"Now I wasn't one of the working girls, but I busted my butt in her kitchen. How did you serve up six hundred? That's something I just don't get."

Gail and Lola wandered up the deck, winding around the parked helicopters like they were briar patches, and ducking under shroud tie-downs as if they were kudzu vines.

And as they walked and talked, Gail's world felt as if it wasn't quite as irrational as she'd thought it was.

# # #

"This is crazy." Sly meant to mutter it to himself two days later, but that didn't work when you were wearing a helmet and were plugged into a comm circuit.

"What is? Everything looks okay here," Dave was watching his engine readouts closely.

They were taking the LCAC out for a spin to check her engines after the latest tune-up. He also wanted some more practice running blind at night. For a load, he'd driven the three M-ATVs back aboard, an easy forty tons, about two-thirds capacity for the LCAC. Sly liked keeping his craft and his skills at a hundred percent capability.

The waves had built up a half-meter taller than the run to the Ivory Coast and the moon was still down. He had his running lights on, but kept the big floods off so that he could concentrate on the feel rather than the look of what he was doing.

"We're on course and flying true," Tom reported. Not that Nav was being especially tricky on this run. Go that way for a while. Do some sliding turns in the two-meter ocean rollers. Come back. Don't run anyone over going either way. Not much chance of that. The carrier group had departed for the Mediterranean once the resupply was complete. *Peleliu* once again cruised alone off the West African coast awaiting orders.

"Idiots!" Nina muttered over the comm from her outpost in the port-side tower. "He's talking about the girl."

"I'm not talking about the girl!" Sly insisted, knowing it was too late.

"What girl?" Dave and Tom spoke practically in unison.

Jerome was down in the engine spaces. He'd be on headset, but the man never spoke unless something broke, which Sly could really appreciate at the moment.

"You guys. Getting me wet here Sly," Nika reported excess spray on her windshield. "These are what you call friends? You really need an upgrade, man."

Actually he thought he was doing pretty well counting the three of them as both his closest friends aboard and as his crew.

"Oh," Tom turned as if he were trying to look back over his shoulder to the empty observer's seat.

"What girl?" Dave asked again, still lost as usual. He was one hell of a mechanic, right over into ridiculous nerd status. The sort of guy that if someone said he built his first NASCAR engine as a kindergarten project you had to think twice. He could tune an engine up so sweet that there was nothing like it. It was the rest of the world that was a mystery to him.

"Omelette lady. Pasta lady. Southern fried chicken lady. The one who makes you want to re-up just so you can keep eating her food," Tom clued Dave in. "That one."

By the dim lights of their instruments, Sly could see Dave lean forward to look at him around Tom, "Really?"

"Why do you think he's always running off the 'check out' something?" Nika scoffed. "Straight to the galley, is my guess. You gotta learn some subtle, man."

"Thanks. Little late on that advice."

"You getting any?" Dave asked in a confidential whisper which also didn't work at all over the comm headset.

"Shaddup, Dave!" Sly knew the instant he said it, he'd put too much heat behind it.

Nika snorted.

"That answers that question, doesn't it?" Tom kept his attention on their whereabouts.

Sly risked taking his left hand off the controls for a moment so that he could punch Tom's arm.

"Wow," Dave said softly.

Sly concentrated on angling the hovercraft another five degrees to port so that he took the waves more to starboard. Nope. Five to starboard worked better. He tried a cross-control so that they kept moving in a straight line, just rotated five degrees to the side. He fed a little more power to the starboard side blower to create more lift on that side. That actually had possibilities. He tried it again at two-and-a-half. Nope. Back to five.

"So, what's the problem?"

"There's no problem," Sly cut a hard turn hoping to change the subject, knowing it wouldn't work. Nika was tenacious as hell, that was a key element of what she brought to the team.

Nika sighed in exasperation, "Sly, buddy. Six straight days, eighteen meals you talked about her food. Then the last three days, she just keeps gettin' better and yet you don't say word one. Now that's crazy talk, man. Or crazy lack of talk."

"It's good food," he knew he sounded lame.

"No argument, dude. But come on. What went sideways?"

Sly thought about it.

It was the trip to the aircraft carrier. And it wasn't just the chef who hugged her goodbye either.

They really needed to talk.

# # #

"No. I'm fine."

Lola looked steadily at her and Gail did her best not to fidget. They were in her space, in her galley.

This is where she should be most comfortable, but it wasn't working.

The problem was that Lola hadn't come alone, there were five of them here.

Dinner service was done. Galley clean and crew gone. Midrats crew wouldn't be in for hours. All the lights were out except for the down-lights over the central prep table where they all sat. It has been casual at first. Lola and Trisha had dropped in, supposedly hunting for another round of the night's…morning's… dinner's chocolate mousse.

They'd taken to coming by the galley, or the three of them would go for a run together on the Hangar Deck which offered the largest track area on the ship. She was starting to think she'd found some possible friends on the ship.

By the time they sat down. The Asian-American gunner Kee and her mismatch adopted daughter Dilya had drifted in with the same excuse. Connie, the 5D's genius mechanic, didn't bother pretending she had an excuse; she simply came into the galley and sat down at the huge stainless steel prep table. Thankfully, she chose a stool on Gail's side so it wasn't like she was facing an inquiry board.

Or was it?

"Really, I'm fine."

Lola rolled her eyes, "You're a mess, girl. Trust me, it takes one to know one. It gives me hope."

"I'm not— Wait. What? It gives you hope that I'm a mess?"

"Sure!" Trisha offered one of her big smiles. "If you aren't a train wreck, you aren't allowed in the 5D."

"I'm a Navy chef, not an Army helicopter flyer. I can't be in your revered 5th-battalion D-company."

"That bother anyone here?" Trisha looked up and down the line. "Nope?" She turned back to Gail. "You're outvoted. Honorary 5D member. Done." She pounded the side of her fist on the table like a gavel.

"Uh, is that actually an honor or am I in it even deeper now?"

"Honor." "Oh yeah, absolutely." "Of course it's good."

Connie remained silent.

Dilya, the teenager, did an eye roll toward the others that told Gail she'd been right on the second part of her guess. She was in it way deeper...whatever *it* was.

Maybe if she banged her head on the table for a while this would all go away. She wouldn't bet on it, so she ate another spoonful of chocolate mousse instead. Next time she'd see if she couldn't scare up some seventy-percent dark chocolate and back off on the heavy cream just a little—a half gallon less per batch should be about right.

"There's a tradition among the 5D," Lola began. "We—"

"It's a tradition we're big on," Trisha cut in. "I'm the worst of the lot."

There was a sudden silence as no one argued and Trisha just grinned.

"We," Lola gave Trisha a look that might quell her for the next thirty seconds, might not. "We each have gone through this. Some of us so bad that we were almost kicked out of the 5D. It was a tradition started by the first female pilot of SOAR, Major Emily Beale."

At the mention of her name, the room shifted. The women, every one of them including Dilya grew quiet for a moment.

"Oh, I'm sorry. How did she die?" Probably on some wild 5D mission that they couldn't tell her about. Dumb question.

"She isn't dead."

Which made Gail's question even dumber.

"Worse," Trisha whispered in a loud voice, "she had a kid." Trisha offered a shudder.

Lola and Connie looked a little wistful. They were each married to a crew chief who flew on another helicopter aboard. Trisha had married a D-boy, one of the ones who had slid down out of the little helo onto the embassy's roof.

Kee appeared to be the sort of person not given much to the softer emotions. The only people Kee let in at all were her Air Mission Commander husband and their adopted war-orphan daughter. Even now she and Dilya sat as close together as best friends.

"Back to the point," Lola must have a clear point to try and drag it through this crowd. "We all arrived with, I'll be kind, issues. Frankly I was such a female disaster area that Emily should have just booted my ass—"

Hands went up around the table in agreement.

"—but she didn't. Instead she made it simple. Once you get past all the crap, the question is: do you want in badly enough to fight to stay here?"

All of them turned to look at her.

Her snort of laughter took them aback.

"I don't even know why I'm here to begin with. I have no Special Operations training. I'm a chef. Why did they pick me to come aboard the *Peleliu*? I've figured out enough to know it wasn't random, but it sure isn't making any sense to this girl. Any of y'all can answer that one for me, I'll be right pleased."

By the looks going around, she could tell they didn't.

"I bet Michael knows," Trisha offered up.

"Michael? The D-boy? Why would he know?"

"Michael knows everything," Dilya said softly, speaking for the first time.

Gail opened her mouth, but the others were nodding their agreement.

Gail closed her mouth and focused back on her mousse.

Colonel Michael Gibson of Delta Force was not the man she needed to be talking to.

Chapter 10

S*ly was sitting in* the control room of the LCAC parked in the Well Deck. He should be doing something constructive, but for the life of him he couldn't think of what.

Dave and Tom were seeing to topping off the fuel tanks. Nika was doing the post-op inspection. Someday he was going to count up the number of steps required to prep and shutdown the LCAC. Then he'd go up and check that number with Connie or John Wallace and find out who had more, his craft or one of their helos.

Sly tried to focus on writing his report. He'd learned things about a night run in moderate seas that other craftmasters would find useful, but he couldn't seem to form the words in his head. *Just starting writing your observations and it will come together.*

And stop thinking about the woman.

He had down a decent description of the problem he was trying to solve, best average angle of attack when you couldn't see each individual wave.

Someone was headed up the control room ladder. It wasn't the clatter of Dave or Tom. And Nika only rarely came up to his unofficial office.

It was—

Damn! She took his breath away every time. Like a gut punch, Gail Miller was standing at the head of the ladder and looking at him.

"Hi, Chief," her voice was soft, barely carrying to him across the small space.

"Hi, Chief," he managed back despite the throttlehold someone had around his throat.

"You got a minute?"

He managed a nod and waved her to a chair. Three days since the aircraft carrier. Three days since he'd seen her up on deck, talked to her, talked about her cooking. Longest goddamn days of his life. How in hell had he gotten so far gone on this woman so fast? All that crap about "the right one" that he'd always scoffed at. Is this what it felt like? As if his guts had been trapped on a storm-tossed sea?

She sat in Dave's seat and spun it a quarter-turn to face him, propping her feet on Tom's chair.

He also turned his chair to face her.

It was stupid, but he let himself drink her in. Those long legs wrapped in tan slacks. The t-shirt and sports bra only emphasizing a glorious figure he'd barely begun to know. And those dark eyes that watched him so quietly, the only calm in his own personal storm.

"You said if I needed someone to talk to…"

He managed a nod.

She covered her face with her hands for a moment and then scrubbed at her cheeks before dropping them into her lap.

"I've just been informed that I'm a total mess, and I'm afraid that they're right."

A stupid line came to mind, Sly tried to repress it, but he wasn't having much luck doing that today. "If this is you as a mess, I don't know if I can handle you when you're all put together."

Her smile acknowledged the compliment rather than laughing in his face.

He felt his own grin was a little sheepish, but it was true. The woman simply knocked him out every time. Or at least his brain and his libido which was a more than sufficient damage path.

"I'm sorry I've been avoiding you, but I had some things to figure out. However, I'm no closer to any answers for doing that."

He'd thought he was the one avoiding her. Was it good or bad that she was doing the same?

"I really like you, Sly."

Like? When your woman said *like,* the news was very bad. Awful.

"And the way we feel together…"

Here it comes. She was about to kill him with her words.

She ran a hand back through her hair, "…the word fantastic definitely comes to mind."

Totally… "What?" Had he heard right? Relief threatened to swamp him. "But I thought you and—" he bit his tongue. Too late. Gail Miller had turned him into a bumbling fool; not something he was used to.

"Matheo? No. We do have a past, but he is also one of the closest friends I have. We've known each other since I was three and he was a glorious boy of twelve. And yes, he was just as overwhelmingly handsome then to."

"Why doesn't that make me feel any better?"

"Sly, you have nothing to worry about in that department. I think that's one of my problems. That one night we had here…" She looked over at the observer's chair sitting empty beside them and blushed.

Sly could feel the heat rising to his own cheeks, but did his best to beat it back. He didn't want to remember her there every time he looked at the seat—he wanted to have her there. Wanted to drive her up over some shuddering peak and know that he was the only man who had ever taken her so far, so high.

"I'll just say that you're an amazing lover and I don't know what to do with that either."

He had a few ideas, but he didn't think it would be a wise move to suggest them at the moment.

Her smile said that he was completely transparent to her... as always. He shrugged an acknowledgement.

"But that's not what I need to talk about or why I've been avoiding you."

"Okay," he was impressed that his voice still worked. He set his clipboard on the command console to show that she had all of his attention; which she always did—while he was driving the LCAC, while he was eating, and while he was trying to sleep and not succeeding very well.

"While on the *George H. W. Bush* Matheo gave me a job offer, to be his sous chef."

After the relief of a moment before, the jolt that she could be leaving slammed into him and robbed him of any ability to respond. Thankfully she didn't appear to notice and continued.

"It's the premier mess of the entire Navy," she began idly toggling the lights on the tiny Christmas tree on and off.

Each time it went on, he was reminded of the soft light and shadow it had cast over her naked body as she took and gave in his arms that one morning.

"Sous chef on the newest and biggest aircraft carrier on the planet. Instead of serving six hundred, I'd be cooking for six thousand. He's a masterful chef. He trained me. I'd stand to learn so much more from him."

"He wants you for more than just cooking," Sly ground it out.

"He does," she acknowledged as if it was the most normal thing on the planet, "but that's not why he offered. I don't want to get into his and my past, but it's a past that doesn't necessarily mean there's a future. If I decided to go and only be his assistant, then he'd accept that."

Sly tried to swallow that one down. He'd been so handsome. So boisterously French. And he had hugged Gail like…well, like they had a past, present, and future.

He closed his eyes and could see the scene perfectly.

Breakfast service had wound down by the time he'd come looking for her. Lunch prep was starting up on the heels of the cleaning crew—no break between services on the carrier. The tall chef had wound his arms around Gail cradling her against him, his face buried in her dark red hair.

Gail had been in his arms.

Her own arms around his waist…rather than his neck like a lover.

Her head on his shoulder…but facing away. Not buried into his neck, but turned out like a friend's.

Was she naïve enough to think that if she went aboard the carrier they wouldn't become lovers once again? No. One thing Sly had learned about Chief Miller was that, despite his initial assessment, she saw the world very clearly.

So, if she said this wasn't about her relationship with the chef, he would have to believe her no matter how difficult that was to do. He looked at her once more as the Christmas lights blinked out.

"If you're going to leave any relationship with the chef out of the question, then you must do the same with me. That's why you've been avoiding me."

"No. The reason I've been avoiding you is that if I decide to go, I don't want to hurt you more than I already will." She turned the tree lights back on and finally let go of the switch and pulled her hands back into her lap to clench them together.

"So, all of the unkind thoughts I've had about you and the Frenchie," he said it with the best smile he could dredge up to make it a tease, "were actually you being a kind and decent woman? I have to warn you, Chief. It just makes me like you even more."

"Darn it!" her own smile made it easier. "Not part of my plan."

He felt as if he could breathe for the first time since she'd ascended his ladder.

It hadn't been a one-night stand.

Or not a normal one-night stand. They'd had one night, before the transfer offer had threatened to change her future, and so she'd backed off rather than risking them getting in deeper.

"And you came to me for help?"

She nodded tightly.

What courage had that taken to do? Trusting that he'd understand rather than just being pissed about chef Matheo.

But she did trust him. On top of that, she made him feel as if he was a better man for it. She'd taken it as a given that he'd be decent enough to be of help despite his own involvement.

"And it was either you or the scariest group of women I've ever met."

He burst out laughing. There was no question who she was talking about. The women of the 5D were charming, beautiful, fantastically skilled at their jobs—and scary as all hell.

"Okay. Then let's start at the top. Sous chef on an aircraft carrier versus Chief Steward on an aging LHA."

# # #

Gail was torn between a desire to laugh, cry, or throw herself at Chief Stowell and damn the consequences.

The laughter was the joy that maybe she wasn't in this alone. And the weeping was the relief for the same reason. The throwing herself at the Chief she only resisted because there was still too much unresolved. That, and she could see his crew moving about the hovercraft and occasionally casting glances up in their direction.

Sly was such a good man it was almost unbelievable. She'd come to him out of desperation, not really expecting him to find his way through the bizarre maze that was her life.

But he did.

She told him about the Admiral Ney Award and her desire to create the best mess in Navy.

He asked about what she thought she'd learn not only from Matheo but also from cooking on such a large scale. For comparison, she did her best to guess what she'd learn from running her own mess—granted a smaller one than the LHA posting had led her to anticipate.

That juxtaposition was a hard one and they chased it around as the sun rose and filled the Well Deck with daylight.

As they spoke, Gail could also feel herself relaxing, amazed at how comfortable she was around Sly. Leaning back in opposite seats, she'd finally stretched her legs out with her heels propped on Tom's middle seat. Sly had matched her position, their ankles and feet making a comfortable tangle as they spoke.

Enough of a tangle that they couldn't extricate themselves quickly when the D-boy Colonel, Michael Gibson, appeared at the head of the ladder. She hadn't heard him coming, neither had Sly. One moment he wasn't there, the next he was.

Gail felt the blood rush to her face, though they hadn't been doing anything more than talking and playing a little footsie. Then she felt the blood drain back out when she saw how he was dressed.

He wore full battle gear: helmet, vest with its pockets filled with spare magazines, handgun holstered over his abdomen with another at his side, and a rifle over his shoulder.

He didn't even spare a glance at their feet.

"How fast can we be underway, Chief Stowell?"

Gail glanced out the windows to see Rangers scrambling up the front ramp and onto the LCAC, struggling to shoulder their gear while on the move.

"Fast as I find my crew."

"Here!" "Yo!" Dave and Tom popped up the ladder and started pulling out their vests and helmets.

"Do you have extra gear for Chief Miller?"

"I do."

"Observer's seat," was all he said to her then he was gone.

Tom dropped an armored vest over her head and helped her reset the Velcro side straps for her much smaller frame. Dave handed her a helmet as she moved out of his seat.

"What the—"

"We'll find out. Hear that?" He tipped his head to the side as he turned for his controls.

The *Peleliu's* engines, which had been running at little over an idle, nearly inaudible beneath the background noise of the steel ship. Now they were winding up. Way up. In moments the sound had increased until she could feel it transmitted through the frame of the hovercraft.

"They're already cavitating the propellers. That's hard on them. Whatever it is, they're in a major hurry."

The ship shuddered and leaned as it turned hard, still accelerating as it went.

Gail buckled into her seat and tried to remember to keep breathing.

The helmet was a poor fit, but adjusting the straps made it acceptable. She plugged in the cable that connected her to the communications system in time to hear...

"—Barstowe. Rangers aboard. Good to go."

"Preflight good, ready for 'go' command," Dave spoke up.

"This is *Peleliu*," came a voice she didn't recognize. "LCAC cleared for immediate launch."

"Fire her up, Dave," Sly was settling himself into place. "Raise the gate."

The LCAC engines whined to life.

Gail's pulse rate climbed and she couldn't stop it. She wasn't trained for this.

Welcome to the Navy, honey. Never do the expected.

"You good to go, Chief Miller?"

Just hearing Sly's voice was a huge relief. She tried to speak, she really did, but her voice just wasn't working. So, she leaned forward and patted Sly twice on the shoulder in acknowledgement. Feeling him there—feeling the reality of his strong shoulder so close, and learning to appreciate that inner strength more and more—knocked the panic back enough to finally gasp out, "Good to go."

At Sly's "Do it!" Dave inflated the skirts.

There was no burst of spray like the first time. Gail glanced over at Nika on the opposite side of the craft. Her head was clearly visible behind the thick glass with no windshield wipers needed.

Over her shoulder she spotted a problem, "Ship's rear gate is still closed, Chief."

"Goddamn it!" he keyed the mike. "*Peleliu*, get that damned gate out of my way before I get there."

He had the hovercraft up and sliding backward even as the gate lowered. It was a close thing, but they got it level before the hovercraft arrived. Sly fed the power and the LCAC rushed out into the morning.

Except it wasn't sunny. The sky was overcast and the waves were rough. Still only a meter or so high, but there was chop and they looked wind-torn.

Once out the rear gate, he jogged sideways, then rammed ahead over the *Peleliu's* rising wake.

"Where are we going?"

"Don't know yet," Sly responded. "But the *Peleliu* has settled on this course. Good enough for me. Dave, give me everything the engines have. I'm guessing we're in a bit of a hurry."

Gail was watching the *Peleliu* disappear astern which was the only reason she spotted the D-boy returning silently to the cabin.

"Heads-up!" she warned the crew.

He actually grinned at her, a brief flash that acknowledged he was trouble, then it was gone.

"Hey, Michael," Sly didn't turn but instead remained intent on nursing his craft forward. "What's cooking?"

"Isn't that *your* analogy?" he said to her softly before raising his voice. "We have an airliner on a Johannesburg-London flight declaring an emergency. Major systems failure, they're trying to get her down."

"Oh crap!" Sly cursed. "I can't just park in the mid-Atlantic and pick folks up. That's not what I'm built for."

"They're not coming down in the water. They think they can make Port Bouet Airport."

"Then why are we rushing to their aid?" Gail asked.

The D-boy turned to look at her as Sly answered, his voice grim.

"Because Port Bouet Airport is in the city of Abidjan, Ivory Coast."

Oh great. As if one trip into a battle zone wasn't enough.

# # #

"How bad?" Sly asked and slid the throttles up to the edge of overload.

"Civil unrest in the city has increased since we evacuated the American Embassy. The embassy has been burned. All flights have long since been suspended there, but the local militias will certainly congregate rapidly upon the plane's arrival."

In answer to his next question, the first of the SOAR helicopters shot by low overhead. Two more were close behind it.

"Chief Stowell?" Dave's voice was a whisper over the intercom. "We got a problem."

"Tell me."

"We've got a full load of fuel. It'll get us there, but it won't get us back. The *Peleliu* is too far out. Especially not at the rate we're burning it."

Clearly that's why the *Peleliu* had turned and was racing for the coast. The LCAC was going to die halfway back to safety and it was going to be a challenge to see how many they could keep alive until the ship reached them. There was a storm incoming. Not a big one, no problem for the ship. But it was going to wreak havoc on an LCAC abruptly afloat in the middle of it.

"Chief?" Gail. Her voice sounded steady. Good girl. Proving herself yet again.

"What do you see?" He scanned the horizon because she always saw things so fast it was almost alarming.

"Well, nothing yet. But we are going to an airport, right?"

"Right. So?"

"Your engines are essentially jet engines aren't they."

Sly sighed, "Not a whole lot of people can make me feel slow and stupid, Chief Miller." But she sure did. He should have thought of that himself.

"Glad to help," the laugh was back in her voice. A good sign.

"I don't get it," Dave was still studying his readouts. "We're still going to run out of fuel."

"Careful, Dave," Sly warned him good-naturedly. "Or you'll be the one I send out to steal a fuel truck of Jet A fuel in the middle of a riot."

# # #

Michael looked at her for a moment, offered a nod.

Gail considered. It was less as if he was acknowledging her insight, and more as if he was confirming his own thinking about something.

"I was right about you." Then he was gone.

He was—

And then she remembered where she'd seen Colonel Michael Gibson of Delta Force before, though she'd had no idea that's who he was. It had been years ago on the *Reuben James* where she'd been laughing at a grumpy ship's captain wearing cranberry sauce down his dress whites.

That explained why she was here. Here on a Special Operations Force's ship.

Gibson must have set a pre-request so that when her name had popped up as being available, the system had swept her out to the *Peleliu.*

She'd always heard that the number one qualification for being Special Operations was that you didn't fit in anywhere else. And Delta was the pinnacle of that, the guys were barely controlled renegades to hear most commanders speak of them. "Very effective ones," they would always immediately amend their statement.

She'd always liked the sound of that, but there was no such thing as a Special Operations Chief Steward.

Except now maybe there was.

Because the military's premier soldier had decided that she was exceptional beyond the kitchen.

Something else she didn't need to know.

No pressure!

She looked out the rear window and spotted Gibson moving out onto the deck. Maybe she should go down and ask, but she knew her reasoning was right. Perhaps she should go down and argue with him, point out that he was completely wrong about her.

Except hadn't the lead pilot of the 5D just said that "being a mess" was a necessary qualification? Oh brother.

She saw Michael look up and back behind the LCAC; she did as well.

"Keep it steady, Chief," she called out as one of the SOAR helicopters slid up from behind and twenty meters above them.

"Goddamn it!" A huge wall of spray arced up from over the bow. She watched it slam into Michael, expecting to see him washed up against the rear gate battered and bloody.

Instead, he stood back up from where he must have ducked behind one of the M-ATVs at the last second before the spray had hidden him.

"What happened, boss?" Nika called over the intercom.

"Downdraft from the helo drove my bow down into a wave. I'm compensating now. What's it doing so low?"

Gail watched as a line spun down from the Black Hawk's cargo bay.

Michael walked up to the line and grabbed it as if it wasn't flopping madly about in the wind of the LCAC's passage and the rotor's downdraft. He snapped it to his vest.

Another wave slammed aboard. Michael rose out of the resulting spray headed aloft like an angel on a string—a very heavily armed angel.

"Michael, can you call them off?" Sly was cursing quite impressively.

"Your Navy is showing through, Chief Stowell. Besides, Michael's up there ahead of you."

The three drivers looked up to see the man dangling from the rapidly shortening line as the helicopter shot ahead.

"Where the hell is he going?"

"My guess?" Gail could feel herself smile. Knew she was right. "He's going to go steal a fuel truck."

Chapter 11

W̲hat was a frustrating two-hour trip on the hover-craft was a thirty-minute flight for the helos. Sly hoped to god they'd kept the downed plane safe until he arrived.

He breached the shoreline and roared across the four-lanes of Bassam Expressway without even slowing to look. Cars and trucks veered and dodged. He did his best not to run over anyone.

The rubber skirt could take a great deal of damage before too much air leaked out to provide good lift, but he didn't want to start whatever was coming with it already torn up.

He managed to cross over the big roadside ditch and make it to the airport tarmac.

Which plane was involved was obvious. It was parked in the middle of the runway and a hornet's nest of helicopters swarmed about it shooting at lines of vehicles along the runway and taxiways. Some trucks were burning, sending great plumes of black smoke skyward. A few were flipped. Some sat at an angle that said their tires, or perhaps their whole engines had been shot out.

Stopping here at the outskirts of the airport to off-load the Rangers so that the M-ATVs could join the fray seemed like the best approach.

"No!" Gail called out as soon as he slowed his craft. "All the way in Chief."

He surveyed the layout. No passengers on the ground. Maybe they were tucked away in a terminal somewhere safe, or already captured.

"Talk to me, Gail."

"The plane's doors are still closed. No exit ramps either. They must still be aboard. Get right under the main passenger door in front of the wing."

"Hell of a jump," that door was a dozen meters up in the air. It was an Airbus A380, the biggest jetliner in the world. "I hope to Christ she isn't full."

"They won't be jumping," Gail sounded pretty wound up. "Get right under it, then park nose out and get the Rangers out of the way."

Driving into the middle of a riot wouldn't be his first choice. But she sounded so sure of herself. And he'd overheard Gibson say that he'd been right about her.

Right about how good she was?

It was enough to tip the balance in his mind. So much of a dynamic situation was gut feel and his gut said, "Go!"

He went, swinging wide around the tail and wing.

He radioed his intent up to Lola who acknowledged even as she swooped down to kill another pickup that had found its way through the demolition derby already in place.

Clint Barstowe didn't even respond, he simply got his Rangers loaded. The instant the front gate was down, the three vehicles and the Rangers roared off the ramp.

"This had better be good, woman."

# # #

"Oh, this is good, Chief. Tell the plane to pop their evacuation slide."

When he didn't respond, Gail reached out and nudged Sly hard.

He shook loose from his momentary shock with a laugh. "Goddamn! You are good! I didn't even see it. Flight," he called over the radio, "pop your evac chute. Front door only. Get them down here now."

Gail spun around in her seat to watch; they all did.

The passenger door swung open high above them. Then the giant plastic chute billowed out and inflated. It landed almost perfectly in the center of the LCAC's deck.

Gail popped her seatbelt, grabbed a portable radio, and rushed down the ladder.

The power of the uniform, even if it was a helmet and vest over a t-shirt and standard khakis, put her in charge by the time the second passenger was down the chute. She and the deckhand, Jerome, directed them toward the back of the LCAC's deck area as they slid down.

"Sly," she got on the radio. "Raise the front gate enough that no one tries to run away in panic."

"Also so that a stray bullet doesn't bite your ass."

She hadn't thought of that, "That would be bad." She could feel herself freezing, as panicked as the civilians streaming down the chute toward her.

"Real bad," Sly offered drily. "It's a very cute ass."

That jarred her loose. "You're just biased."

"Damn straight."

She didn't have time to be afraid, so she shoved it aside. Though she was plenty glad when the gate raised enough that she could no longer see the distant mob.

The loud roar of a truck racing toward the hovercraft almost scared the daylights out of her. She was sure they were going to be rammed.

"Hi Michael," Sly called out over the radio. "While you're filling her up, would you mind washing the windows and checking the oil?"

There hadn't been a fuel truck when they pulled up to the plane. That meant Michael had been dropped behind what she could only think of as "enemy lines" and crossed through the battle zone driving a vehicle filled with explosive through an angry mob armed with guns. D-boys were even scarier than she thought.

Soon passengers were packed aboard so tightly there was no room to sit. Strictly standing-room only.

Finally, after what felt like forever, she saw the plane's officers in suits at the head of the ramp and knew they were almost done. Which was good. There was barely going to be enough room for the flight crew. The stewards and then the flight officers slid down; the last one closing the door behind him and latching it, as if that was going to make a difference, before letting gravity sweep him down the chute.

Gail decided that she wouldn't be telling him about the two bullets that passed into the fuselage right where his head had been moments before.

The engines began cycling back up.

"Sly! The Rangers," both the front and the back gates were closed. There might not even be room for the men.

"They're okay. Get back up here."

"I think I'd be of more help down here."

"That's the stewards' and flight officers' jobs. It's going to get rough and I don't want you getting broken. They're trying to fly a medical team down from the carrier, but the storm is much worse up there. Consider it an order."

They might be of similar rank, but he was the craftmaster and that made it an order. You didn't disobey an order and expect to have a career.

Gail looked up at the black clouds. Her visor was covered with spatters of rain. She hadn't even noticed when it started.

The LCAC lurched to life sending the packed crowd stumbling to one side then the other. It was enough mass to rock the hovercraft badly.

She helped raise the plane's emergency chute up over everyone's heads. Eager hands helped, batting it aloft until the hovercraft slid out from underneath. The big opening left behind in the middle of the deck filled quickly with passengers, which eased the pressure on the crowd.

Gail signaled to the flight crew and shouted over the roar of the engines.

"Get them sitting. Pack them as tight as you can. Have them sit with their legs around each other, anything you need to do to brace them, but get them off their feet. Cotton, torn cloth, anything you can get in their ears will help."

Her instructions galvanized the shell-shocked crew into action. In moments, she recognized that she was in the way and began heading for the control tower, signaling people to sit down as she went. A few panicked ones grabbed for her, but a flight steward intervened quickly. They'd been trained in handling panicked civilians, she'd been trained in handling irate diners. And in the Navy, except for the occasional besmirched Captain, those were very rare.

Everyone had assumed because of her helmet and vest that she was far more important than she was, but as it gained her a clear passage back to the cockpit, she wasn't complaining.

# # #

"Here, Chief."

A hand rested on Sly's shoulder for just a moment, but he knew it was Gail's without her needing to tell him. The relief rolled through him like a wave.

As he headed for the beach, he heard her snap her seatbelt closed behind him. Now he could think. Like how to get out of here.

The helicopters and Rangers had performed a military miracle to keep the mob back and retain an open lane back to the beach.

But time was running short…very short.

The Rangers had driven down the field and a twin-rotor Chinook helicopter had swooped in to gather them all up. The three vehicles sat abandoned on the grassy verge and the mob was already moving toward them.

"We can't let that happen." An angry mob with heavy weaponry was not something he wanted close behind him. But there was nothing he could do, so he aimed down the center of the narrowing lane and pushed ahead as fast as he dared.

After he flew past the vehicles, he heard a massive explosion behind him, louder even than the LCAC's engines.

"What the hell?"

"One of the Black Hawks just punched a Ranger vehicle. I think that was a Hellfire missile. There's nothing left. Two more!" she called a warning.

He heard the double *Krump!* even as the shock wave caught them and threatened to nose him down into the ditch at the field's perimeter. He managed to keep the nose up and make it over the highway and to the beach. Now they were out on the water, which made it both better and worse.

Dave kicked on the windshield wipers against the storm's rain.

The helicopters were moving out ahead of him. They'd be back aboard the *Peleliu* long before he could get there. The only way the folks on the hovercraft's deck were going to survive the ride to safety was if he took it slow. Thirty knots max compared with the eighty he'd run at to get here. Now it would be a dance of speed and fuel, even more than passenger safety.

Despite the darkness of the storm, a brilliant light reflected off the inside of his windscreen. He didn't dare turn away to look, it was taking all of his concentration to crawl out through the breakers.

"What was that?"

"The plane," Gail's tone was an awed whisper. "Why would SOAR blow up the plane?"

Sly sighed, "They wouldn't trash it. That was a four hundred million dollar piece of equipment. The M-ATVs were only a half million each. The plane was probably blown up by some idiot with an AK-47 who took a pot shot and hit a wing tank wrong."

# # #

Gail watched the column of fire that reached up into the cloud layer until it disappeared astern.

Then she looked back down at the miserable passengers below. Instead of deplaning at Heathrow and complaining about how long it takes to unload luggage, they were going to arrive soaked to the bone inside a steel ship of war.

"I—" she turned to face forward once more and decided it would be better if she kept her mouth shut. She was so far out of her depth here. She didn't belong no matter what Colonel Gibson thought.

Windshield wipers slapping side to side were barely keeping the windows clear. Dave and Tom were conferring quietly over load, speed, and fuel calculations.

"What?" Sly asked her.

She shook her head and then realized how utterly useless that was while sitting behind him.

"Nothing."

"What?" Sly repeated a little more firmly.

"I'm feeling pretty damn useless. I'm a chef. I shouldn't be here."

"Shit!" was Nika's response over the intercom. "You're the reason half those folks are alive. Dumping the slide right onto the deck was a totally righteous move."

"But—"

"Own it, girl."

She wasn't saying it right. Gail knew she'd helped. But it was pure chance she'd done anything right. She was a chef in a battle zone.

Sly remained quiet.

It took a moment, but then she understood why. He was being decent...again. He knew her future career was in the balance and that she didn't know which way to go or what she wanted. And he didn't want to weigh in on that. Didn't want to influence her decision with his own personal preferences.

Gail stared back out the window.

She could see the shocks ripple through the crowd as the hovercraft slammed into wave after wave.

At least it was a warm rain, but they'd view that as a small favor.

Well, she knew one thing she could do.

"Tom, can patch me through to the *Peleliu?*"

"Okay, you're patched."

She called in her request.

# # #

Sly met the racing *Peleliu* before he ran out of fuel, but it was a close thing.

The high load and heavy wave action had combined to chew up almost nine thousand gallons of fuel. If Gail hadn't connected that they could refuel at the airport, a real *Duh!* moment for him, and Michael hadn't braved the mob to steal the fuel truck, it would have been a disaster. They'd have been ditched miles out to sea in weather bad enough to swamp them and possibly sink them.

As it was, he made it up the steel beach, inside the *Peleliu*, and managed to settle the hovercraft down. The buck and roll of the ship was enough to slap him side to side of the Well Deck, but they were home. The passengers were safe; at least the ones who'd survived the journey.

He collapsed back in his seat and peeled his helmet as Dave shut down the engines.

"Fumes," Dave mumbled. "I swear, we made it on the fumes of fumes."

"Well, that sucked," Tom dropped the front gate until it landed on the garage ramp then scrubbed at his face.

"How bad is it?" Sly couldn't get out of his seat to look. "How many did I kill?"

"Don't know," Nika spoke from her position atop the port control tower sounding as weary as he felt. "You'd have to ask her."

"Who?" but Sly turned and saw that the observer's chair was empty, the vest and helmet had been laid across the seat.

He staggered to the window, sore and stiff from the extended passage. He looked down and had to blink a couple times to make sense of what he was seeing.

At the head of the ramp was a long table on one side and a huge stack of blankets on the other. Each passenger was helped to their feet and guided up the ramp. One person wrapped a blanket over their shoulders and another placed a steaming cup of soup in their hands.

Gail.

Soup personally served by Chief Miller with her entire team rallied behind her.

All he could do was watch the miracle of it as people were guided out. He assumed they were being led to bunks that had once been occupied by the Marine Expeditionary Unit.

A med crew was moving about the hovercraft's deck, but they had yet to pull a blanket over someone's face. He saw arms and legs being splinted, an IV here and there, but no bodies. Gail's idea of having them sit in long lines with their legs around each other had saved them the battering Sly had so feared.

He knew he should go help, but he was too drained. He'd never fought the LCAC for nine straight hours, and never through such weather. That might be a first for this class of craft. He should record this mission for the other LCAC craftmasters while the experience was still fresh.

Instead, he stood at the window and simply watched. He couldn't look away until the spectacle was done and his boat once more sat empty, parked in the Well Deck with the *Peleliu's* stern gate raised against the storm.

Dozens had left his deck on stretchers, but not one beneath a shroud despite the rough ride.

His crew had been helping. Only he was numb past the ability to respond.

Tom came up and gave him a nudge to get him moving. Dave called from below to make sure Sly had a good grip on the ladder as he went down each rung.

Nika and Jerome met him at the front ramp and the five of them walked back up the steel beach and onto the ship together.

Gail waited for them. She served each one as Tanker wrapped a blanket over their shoulders. Unnoticed, his body was shivering with exhaustion.

He came last and stopped a foot from Gail.

Sly didn't take the cup of soup she offered.

He just looked at her and knew he was really, really screwed.

He'd never been in love before. Often doubted he'd recognize the feeling if it ever happened.

Well, he'd been wrong.

He knew exactly what it felt like.

Love felt like looking into Chief Gail Miller's eyes and watching the smile slowly bloom on her lovely face.

Chapter 12

It was two days before Gail slept. The demands on her galley jumped from eighteen hundred meals a day to thirty-six hundred. Six hundred people had been aboard that flight and all but three had been released from the med bay.

The ship hadn't enough crew in any department for this level of occupation, especially not occupied by civilians who were far more likely to get into trouble as they grew bored and curious. The Flight Deck and command superstructure were closed to them for security reasons. For lack of anything better to do they gathered in the messes at the strangest hours of the day and night.

She ran two full shifts: they fed the *Peleliu's* standard crew through the night, followed by three meals for the rescued plane passengers and flight crew through the day. Gail split her team in two and recruited anyone who could cook without hurting themselves.

The focus?

Comfort food.

By limiting her own crew to work a maximum of four meal services a day out of the six, they were at least still functioning. But she had meal planning to do, unskilled but willing assistants to train and watch out for, supplies to pull, and a hundred other tasks.

She was sitting in her tiny Chief Steward's office trying desperately to remember why she'd come in here in the first place when she became aware of someone watching her. A glance up and what little nervous energy had been sustaining her drained away.

Gail slumped down in her chair and looked up at Sly Stowell leaning against the door jamb.

"Hi, Chief."

"Chief." She couldn't even manage the "Hi." He looked so good leaning there as if *lazy* was a God-given right.

She remembered how he'd looked after the harrowing crossing of the stormy Gulf of Guinea. Rather, how he'd looked at her. The man had been weaving with strain and exhaustion, and wearing the goofiest smile she'd ever seen. She'd managed to set down his cup of chicken noodle soup before he'd folded her in his arms.

He didn't kiss her. Sly had simply folded her against him and held on as if she were his only lifeline in a storm.

It had been different, so different. When Matheo did the same thing, she always felt comfortable, welcome, desired. In Sly's arms she found all of those, and one more…that she still didn't have the words for. Safe was as close as she could come, but it was too mild a word for so rich and nuanced a feeling. It was like describing Hubert Keller's Beef Bourguignon as "stew." There was no place else she'd ever been that felt quite that way.

"Hi, Chief." Was she repeating herself? Might be. But he looked so delicious that…

"Okay, you're done."

"I'm what? No. I—"

"If you can tell me what you came in here for, you can stay." He wore a grin knowing full well her mind was a blank.

Nothing on her desk looked familiar. Lists and lists that she recognized as her own handwriting but she could make no sense of. She tried desperately to focus her eyes, her thoughts, her emotions—no luck.

"So done," he took her hand and tugged her to her feet.

When he did so, she realized it was a good thing he had because she couldn't have done it on her own.

"Time for you to hit the rack."

Rack time. That sounded good. Except she didn't feel tired. Her mind was racing, it just no longer had a recipe to follow, so it was wandering aimlessly.

Tanker was at the prep table, overseeing a half dozen of the regular staff and a trio of home cooks who had showed both aptitude and energy despite their recent ordeal. There was something she had to say to him, but she had no idea what.

He looked at her, spoke…and she didn't understand a single word.

Corridor.

Ladderway.

Another corridor.

Trisha and Dilya playing an intense game of Scrabble somewhere she couldn't connect. Trisha's bright laugh when she looked at Gail.

A door.

To her berth.

The only thing that connected the kaleidoscope of images was Sly's hand guiding her. The only thing still grounding her on this planet was the feel of him, the rich smell of him—a fragrance she wondered if she could find a way to bottle and keep in her sock drawer for special days.

Looking down at her bunk.

Looking down at Sly squatting at her feet as he removed her boots.

"Stay," she whispered.

He looked up at her slowly.

She could see the need, the desire flash hot across those deep, dark eyes, and then slip away like the closing of an oven door.

"You're in no condition to—"

"Stay. Please." She remembered the sunrise. The light sliding into the Well Deck, into the hovercraft as softly as he'd slid into her. She remembered how Sly had made her feel. Back then she'd barely known the man. Now, she knew him better.

Yesterday, no, three days ago, she'd seen him magnificent. For nine long hours, fighting every single wave of the increasing storm to create the smoothest, safest passage. Tirelessly giving everything he had to save his passengers, and he had. He'd given until he'd practically fainted in her arms, but still he'd been last off his craft, unwilling to leave sooner.

How could *that* man make her feel?

"Gail, I—"

"I may be exhausted, but I'm not stupid. I know what I'm asking."

He studied her closely.

"Stay."

# # #

Sly finished undressing Gail and got her down under the covers.

He burned with a desperate need for this woman. Over the last two days, once he'd slept sixteen hours straight, he'd checked in on her as often as possible. She had created stews, pastas, Southern-fried chicken, even goddamn brownies like one of those fairy godmothers in *Cinderella* until the whole ship was permeated with glorious smells of home.

On top of that she'd saved people, saved lives.

Someone save him from taking advantage of her in her present state.

But where she should be passed out, she had instead moved to the far side of the narrow bunk and folded down a corner of the sheet to welcome him. Her long slender arm and bare shoulder promised what else lay hidden so near by.

Rather than closing her eyes, she was watching him, steadily, rationally, without the disoriented madness of exhaustion that she'd exhibited on the way here.

What was a man supposed to do?

Sly knew a gentleman would turn and leave. But he wasn't. He was a man who had looked into the eyes of the woman he loved and seen her looking back at him with such joy that he hardly recognized himself.

Slowly—feeling as if he were floating just above the ocean on a cushion of air but ever so stable and solid—he undressed, turned out the light, and slid in beside her.

She smelled of every recipe she'd made these last days. Not stale spices and flavors, but a rich warmth that satisfied yet teased, a lush taste to her kiss that spoke of zest for life and joy.

He tasted, sampled, and eventually, devoured.

Soft moans rippled down her length. Hands guided, strong fingers held on, dug in as he sent her soaring until her body skittered like a hovercraft, then crashed like a storm. Waves rushed over her so intensely that he could feel them against his lips, his hands, his body.

He kept her aloft, not letting her settle, not even when she begged him to end it.

Would they have another time together? Or would she go to the carrier?

He didn't know.

Would he ever find another woman like her?

That was an easy and emphatic "No."

Could he make her feel even a tenth the joy he felt just watching her do the simple task of feeding scared and battered civilians?

He did his level best.

When he finally gave in to her pleading, found some protection, and drove into her, the results were galvanic. She bucked and clung and groaned until on a final wave that shattered them both, she slammed into peace as abruptly as if entering the Well Deck coming out of the storm.

For a moment he was afraid he'd hurt her or worse, so violent had been the change from storm-tossed lover to peace.

Then she did the craziest thing.

He was still buried deep inside her. Her arms were looped around his neck but no longer holding on.

She shifted just enough the her lips were near his ear.

"Thanks, Chief."

It was the barest whisper before she was asleep in his arms.

Sly shifted and held her a long time while she slept on his shoulder.

Love didn't begin to describe what he was feeling for this woman.

He twisted just enough to kiss her on top of the head and whispered to her before he too fell asleep.

"You're welcome, Chief."

Chapter 13

G*ail woke alone, uncertain* if she remembered what she thought she remembered. She'd been so out of it that it was possible she'd imagined the whole thing. Two things convinced her that it had really happened.

One, her body felt so glorious that mere sleep didn't begin to explain it.

Two, the note atop her neatly folded clothes: *Good morning, Chief.* No smiley face. No goofy little heart. Just a hundred percent pure Sly Stowell.

She showered, with no real idea what time it was, and headed for the galley.

Which Tanker promptly threw her out of.

She found herself standing out in the Officer's Mess holding a tray with blueberry waffles, a fruit compote, and a mug of coffee; feeling horribly disoriented.

Someone waved at her. Trisha.

Gail wandered over and settled at the table occupied by the rest of the SOAR women.

"Good morning, sleepyhead."

"Morning, Trisha."

"Boy, you let someone stay awake for three straight days and look what happens to them. A perfectly respectable Chief Steward sleeps right through five meal services." Trisha's wink on "respectable" was broad, knowing, and...friendly.

"Did they do okay?"

"Are you serious, girl?" Lola scoffed. "They wouldn't dare not live up to your standard. I checked in on them once or twice. They worship the ground you cook on and would never let you down."

There was some deeper message there. Something past Lola's merry tone.

Team. She'd wanted to build her galley into a Navy team. There was so much more that she wanted to do, but that much she'd already done.

"It's more than that, isn't it?" Gail couldn't quite wrap her mind around it. Maybe she was still fuzzy from sleep, but she didn't think that was it.

The various women looked at her as if she wasn't making sense.

Except for Lola. She nodded as if she knew exactly what Gail was talking about.

Which was good because she didn't.

"Building a team, even like this motley crew," the affection for her fellow fliers was clear in her voice, "that takes something special. Emily Beale gave me a vision. No... She gave me the ability to see a vision that was already mine. That's what you bring to your team, the best thing that you can bring. A vision and a belief that it is worth achieving."

There was a sudden silence along the table. Connie nodded, as did Dilya. Kee offered a non-committal shrug which Gail had learned meant she probably agreed.

Trisha leaned her head on her commander's shoulder and gave her a one-armed hug. "We love you too, boss."

Lola made a fist and bumped the side of it lightly on top of Trisha's bright red hair.

"Of course," Lola turned back to Gail, "that's one of the problems of building a team. Then you have to put up with them."

"Psychosis is a two-way street," Trisha acknowledged around a fresh mouthful of waffle. "We get to give back as good as we get."

Give back as good as we get?

Gail had certainly gotten, and not just from her crew. There was a certain Chief Stowell that she had to track down for he had certainly given to her. He'd given her patience, and strength, and...

She could feel the blood drain from her face.

"Quite something when it finally catches up with you?"

"What?"

Lola was leaning her elbow on the table with her chin in her hand. The rest of the table were talking about Emily Beale. Lola simply quirked up an eyebrow and smiled at her.

Gail couldn't catch her breath.

Sly hadn't just given her good feelings. He'd given her...

"Uh huh. I know that look. Seen it in the mirror. It's quite something," Lola reached out to pat Gail's hand in comfort. "Don't let it scare you. It will make sense eventually."

She certainly hoped so, because at the moment, it most certainly didn't.

Chief Petty Officer Sly Stowell had given her his love.

And as the good Lord on high knew, she didn't have a clue what to do with it.

# # #

Tanker let her back into her own galley for lunch and dinner, had to because she'd ordered him to go and get some sleep. But by the time it was the end of her normal day, he threw her back out before the plane's passengers came sniffing around for their own breakfast.

So, at loose ends, she'd tracked down Sly. It hadn't been hard. Within minutes of the end of dinner service, he just happened to be standing in the corridor outside the galley chatting with Nika, though neither of them would normally have an excuse to be on this deck.

Nika departed with an eye roll and a grin.

Without a word, she led Sly back to her cabin. This time, the taking care of each other's needs was wholly mutual.

She wanted to give back as good as she'd gotten…but *love?* That was a word she wasn't in the least ready to wrestle with. So she wrestled with his body instead and received no complaints.

When they were both sated beyond the ability to do anything more than curl up together, she lay in her favorite position; her head on his shoulder, her palm spread over the center of his chest where she could feel both the powerful muscles and the beating of his heart against her palm.

"Carrier group is clear of the storm. We should be meeting up with them tomorrow. Plan is to trans-ship all of the passengers. The carrier will deliver them to Dakar to catch a ride home."

"That's good. We simply aren't staffed for this big a crew."

He slid his hand up and down her back, sending warm tingles through her that made her sigh with contentment.

"You could transfer with them."

The heat of a moment before turned to a chill.

Gail clicked on a small reading light and propped herself up on one elbow to look down at Sly.

He looked away, but not as if he was uncomfortable. Instead he let his eyes follow his hand as it traced a line of fire down her neck, along the curve of her collarbone, and finally down to trace the curve of her breast. The lightness of his touch, the contrast of so much gentleness from such strong, calloused hands, sent shivers shooting through her. Shivers of heat battling the cold that had clamped about her heart at his words.

"Did you really just say that?"

"You still haven't decided, have you?"

She…hadn't. "Darn it! You aren't supposed to be able to see inside me like that."

"Obvious male opportunity to tell you how much I enjoy *being* inside you." He brushed a kiss over her lips.

"Instead you're just going to just keep fondling my breast like that so that I can't think?"

"No, Chief. Instead, I'm going to do this so that you can't think." He replaced his hand with his mouth and slid his hand down between her legs.

As her mind blanked, she knew at least one part of the answer. She'd never again be able to go back to Matheo. There simply wasn't another lover like Sly Stowell.

# # #

Gail sat in her office and contemplated her latest inventory. She'd finished a resupply request and was wondering if she'd missed anything. The *Peleliu's* stores had just served double meals for four straight days, it was foolish not to restock with the freshest supplies she could requisition while the carrier group and her supply ships were in the area.

She checked the calendar. December 23rd. Tomorrow was Christmas dinner and she'd done absolutely no planning for the biggest shipboard meal of the year.

The days had slid by. She'd been aboard three weeks, it felt like three days.

Except it didn't.

She'd made friends here. Lola and Trisha had become less scary. Gail would wager that the others would as well with time.

She had come to know her ship and her crew. Leaving them would be awfully hard.

And then there was…

Gail looked up and there he was, once more leaning against her doorway as if it was exactly where he belonged.

And then there was Sly Stowell.

Impossibly, as simply as that, she knew her answer to so many questions.

She kicked out a bottom desk drawer and propped her feet up on it as she studied his face. It was a face she knew so well already. One that she looked forward to getting to know far better in the future.

"If I'm going to stay on this ship…"

Sly went very still.

"…and stay with you…"

It appeared he'd stopped breathing. She was half tempted to pause and see if he turned blue. But she resisted.

"…there is one major issue we're going to have to resolve."

"What's that?" his voice was tight, little more than a brief rumble.

In answer, she added one more item to her requisition list and handed it over to him.

He read down to the bottom of the list.

Then he aimed that sideways smile at her and just melted her heart.

Chapter 14

S*ly and his crew* had really done it up. Gail had never seen anything quite like it.

She crossed down from the vehicle garage and stood at the head of the garage ramp where she'd done her soup kitchen service. At the foot of the ramp sat the LCAC with its front and rear gates down.

Twinkle lights and Christmas garlands had been strung from the steel structure of the underside of the Hangar Deck. The hovercraft's deck sported dozens of tables, most made of supply cases of one sort or another, each overlaid with red-and-white checked tablecloths.

Dave had made tiny wire Christmas trees for the middle of each table.

Gail looked up at the LCAC's control tower and could see her little Christmas tree aglow in the window. She was getting very possessive about certain things, but now that she knew she would be staying here, that was okay. There had been nothing to become attached to at SUBASE Bangor or the *Reuben James* before that. In sharp contrast, aboard the *Peleliu* there was so much to get attached to.

And in three-and-a-half short weeks, she had become so.

She crossed through the LCAC and descended onto the planking of the Well Deck. Games had been set up here, darts, ping-pong, several foosball tables had been dug out of the 02 Deck recreation area and brought down. It was shortly after dawn, end of shift for most of the crew.

Jerome and Nika were taking on Tom and Dave at an air hockey table. Sly stood watching them.

"Why aren't you playing?" she asked as she came up beside him.

Sly smiled down at her. "I think that making my living as pilot of a hundred-ton air hockey puck has spoiled me for the game."

Down one side of the Well Deck, Tanker and her crew were setting up a long table of all the trimmings: baked beans, coleslaw, fried corn bread, stewed sweet potatoes, sheet pans over heaters of baked mac and cheese…

The crew had really gone all out. She'd done the major brush strokes, helped each chef tune their seasoning and production methods—there were still six hundred souls aboard after all—but each chef had really owned their own dish. She couldn't be prouder of them.

The rear ramp of the *Peleliu* had been lowered, tilted down into the once-again calm, warm seas. Sailors, male and female, were diving off the steel beach. A fierce game of water polo was raging back and forth across the ocean's surface.

And to either side of the very stern end of the Well Deck were the two big barbeque grills. Hers was to starboard, Sly's to port. Each had a vat of sauce that was cooking on the back corner.

The supply ship did indeed have fresh-butchered hogs—the Navy really did try to put out for those stuck onboard over Christmas. She and Sly had each taken over a grill and spent much of the day tending their individual hogs. By unspoken agreement, they'd done no tasting of the other's preparation.

On a third grill, they spread out chicken quarters, half with her sauce, half with his.

"*Ma bien-aimée!*" Matheo Chastain's call gave her little warning before being wrapped in a bear hug.

She returned it happily, and wondered that it was now no more than the embrace of a dear friend. It had been distilled of all other meaning by a Chief Petty Officer from, God help her, *North* Carolina.

Matheo stepped her back but kept his large hands on her shoulders as he inspected her. "So, it is as I feared. Who is he?"

"That would be me," Sly stepped up beside her.

Matheo clasped Sly's hand with both of his. "Now this is a man lucky beyond price." Then he dropped Sly's hand and turned to the inspect the grills.

Sly looked at her in surprise.

She offered a shrug in return, "Food is always his top priority."

This was Matheo. There was no one else like him. And while she appreciated him, he was not the man for her. Why it had taken so many years for her to know that was a question she wasn't going to ask.

"I hear that you order up hogs and I know I must come taste. I must see what *ma cherie* does. Though why you cook dinner with the rising of the sun; it is still *le mystère.*"

"This one is mine," Gail dipped a ladleful of sauce from the steel canister on the back of the grill, and slathered it over the chicken, then more on the pork. "The other is Sly's."

Matheo turned back to Sly. "So, that is how you catch her heart? She whose heart is always been held so safe. You cook that good?"

Sly looked thoroughly flummoxed so Gail rescued him.

"I don't know. I haven't tasted his food yet."

"Ah. But I can tell there is still no hope for me." He offered a great heaving sigh. "I must taste these."

He reached out and Sly pushed his hand aside.

Matheo looked at him.

"Cooks don't eat before their crew."

Matheo laughed and hugged Sly and pounded him on the back, "Oh, *bien-aimée!* I see why this one you like so much. The straight arrow. He is of course right."

And Matheo pitched in and helped with the service as the crew of the *Peleliu* streamed by the laden tables, filled their plates at the grills, and moved to the picnic tables on the LCAC or sat down on the steel beach.

Lola stood near Gail's grill while tasting the pork. "Oh, girl," she sighed with closed eyes. "Oh. You are doing the South proud today."

Gail felt terribly chipper that her new-found friend so approved. Near the end she was worried that there wouldn't be enough. But finally—after the last plates were filled to be run up to the on-duty watch crew—she, Sly, Matheo, and some of the officers from the carrier—who'd come over to help coordinate the off-loading of the plane's passengers—landed at one of the LCAC's tables. Dave's little Christmas tree lit their table cheerily as they all dug in.

"*Merde!* but this is so good!" Matheo licked where sauce had dribbled down his hand.

Gail sat opposite Sly. By silent mutual consent, they'd each taken the other's barbeque. She bit in and savored.

"I really want to scoff at this, Sly. I really, really do."

Sly's smile acknowledged that she couldn't. And the way his eyes closed as he ate hers left her with no doubt of how much he enjoyed it.

"It doesn't solve our problem, does it?"

"No," she agreed. "I still can't tell you which is better."

"I can," one of the officers spoke up and they all turned to look at him. He glanced over at his companion who nodded his agreement.

"What? Which one?"

"The USS *Peleliu*."

She looked at Sly.

If there was some joke here, he didn't get it either.

The officer looked to Matheo. "You, sir, are very lucky that this mess is in the 'Large Afloat' category, rather than the 'Aircraft Carrier' category."

Matheo opened his mouth and then closed it again looking deeply chagrined, but nodded his head in agreement.

The officer leaned forward to look around Matheo. "We've been eating your food for two days, Chief Miller. I shouldn't say this yet, but there is absolutely no contest anywhere in the 'Large Afloat.' Despite the adverse conditions of an overwhelmed staff and galley due to your unexpected passengers, you keep an exceptional mess. And to top it off with this…" he raised a chicken drumstick dripping with sauce.

One of hers she noted with some pleasure that she'd tease Sly about later.

"…this is some of the best food I've ever eaten. In or out of the Navy."

Gail looked at the officer and his companion but couldn't seem to make sense of the words. There was something she was missing.

Sly kicked her under the table and mouthed, "Admiral Ney Award."

Gail looked back at the grinning officers as it registered. She searched for a response.

She really did.

The one that slipped out surprised her as much as it did everyone else at the table—all of whom burst out laughing.

"Holy shit!"

# # #

Sly sat at the head of the *Peleliu's* stern ramp and watched the sunset. The lazy waves sloshed up and down the steel beach with a soft murmur. The Christmas party had run through most of the day despite it being everyone's "night."

A late mail call had reached the carrier and great bundles of packages and letters from home had arrived at the *Peleliu* adding to the merriment.

Gail's crew had made a vast number of pumpkin, apple, and pecan pies, all of which had been consumed.

And now, at long last, the Well Deck was quiet. And clean, this was the Navy after all, and they were always on call.

He didn't need to hear her to feel her when she approached.

Gail sat down close beside him and laced an arm through his.

"That was some fine barbeque, Chief," she whispered it like a secret.

"Damn good, Chief," he acknowledged.

"I didn't get you a Christmas present, Sly. But I did find a couple of these in ship's stores." She held out a pair of candy canes.

He accepted one with all due grace and they both unwrapped them and began to lick the red and white stripes. They paused for a peppermint kiss that was as good as any he'd ever had in his life.

"I got you something."

"Oh, man," she sighed.

"You say it that way, it doesn't sound like much of a complaint."

"A girl does like a good present. It's not something big is it? I'll be bummed if you got me something big."

"No," he assured her. "Not big. Quite small really." He went back to sucking on his candy cane and watching the sunset turn the wave tips gold.

"Okay, Chief. Give."

"Are you sure?"

"Yes."

"Really sure?" God he so loved teasing this woman.

"Yes!"

He reached into his pocket and pulled out the contents of the package that had arrived for him in this morning's late mail call. He'd been waiting all day for a moment alone with Gail to give it to her.

He kept his hand closed.

"Okay, that's pretty small," she acknowledged. "Smaller than the candy cane I gave you. I can work with that without feeling too awful."

He opened his palm and waited for her to look down.

Sly heard the small gasp.

"It was my grandmother's. I asked Mama to express ship it out…Will you marry me, Gail Miller?" Not the most elegant words, but he figured asking her plain and simple was the best way. It's what fit her.

She looked up at him, studied him with those eyes he always got so lost in. So lost that he'd never be able to find his way back.

Then she looked back down at the ring.

He wondered if she'd been struck speechless. Or if she'd swear again as she had over the Admiral Ney Award, though they'd both been told it was Top Secret-classified until the official announcement. Which had only made it all the more real.

Then Gail looked back up into his eyes. And that smile, which had bowled him over the first moment and left his butt soaking wet, shone brightly upon him.

She held up her hand for him to slide on the ring.

"I will."

He slipped the ring on her finger and leaned in to kiss his peppermint-flavored fiancé.

"Thanks, Chief."

He couldn't have said it better himself.

About the Author

M. L. Buchman has over 30 novels in print. His military romantic suspense books have been nominated for the RT Reviewer's Choice of the Year award, and been named Barnes & Noble and NPR "Top 5 of the year" and Booklist "Top 10 of the Year." In addition to romance, he also writes thrillers, fantasy, and science fiction.

In among his career as a corporate project manager he has: rebuilt and single-handed a fifty-foot sailboat, both flown and jumped out of airplanes, designed and built two houses, and bicycled solo around the world. He is now making his living as a full-time writer on the Oregon Coast with his beloved wife. He is constantly amazed at what you can do with a degree in Geophysics. You may keep up with his writing by subscribing to his newsletter at www.mlbuchman.com.

Bring On the Dusk

the story of the USS Peleliu *and her crew*
contine as Colonel Michael Gibson
finds true love (coming March 2015)

There were few times that Colonel Michael Gibson of Delta Force appreciated the near-psychotic level of commitment displayed by terrorists, but this was one of those times. If they hadn't been, his disguise would have been much more difficult.

The al-Qaeda terrorist training camp deep in the Yemeni desert required that all of their hundred new trainees dress in white with black headdresses that left only the eyes exposed. The thirty-four trainers were dressed similarly but wholly in black making them easy to distinguish. They were also the only ones armed which was a definite advantage.

Their dress code made for a perfect cover. The four men of his team were dressed in loose-fitting black robes like the trainers. Lieutenant Bill Bruce wore dark contacts to hide his blue eyes and they all had rubbed a dye onto their hands and wrists, the only other uncovered portion of their bodies.

Michael and his team had parachuted into the deep desert last night and traveled a quick ten kilometers on foot before burying themselves in the sand along the edges of the main training grounds. Only their faces were exposed, each carefully hidden by a thorn bush.

The mid-day temperatures had easily blown through a hundred and ten degrees. It felt twice that inside the heavy clothing and lying under a foot of hot sand, but uncomfortable was a way of life in "The Unit" as Delta Force called itself, so was of little concern. They'd dug deep enough so that they weren't simply roasted alive, even if it felt that way by the end of the motionless day.

It was three minutes to sunset, three minutes until the start of Maghrib, the fourth scheduled prayer of the five that were performed daily.

At the instant of sunset the *muezzin* began chanting *adhan,* the call to prayer.

Thinking themselves secure in the deep desert of the Abyan province of southern Yemen, every one of the trainees and the trainers knelt and faced northwest toward Mecca.

After fourteen motionless hours—less than a dozen steps from a hundred and thirty terrorists—it was a challenge to make his movement smooth and natural as he rose from his hiding place. He shook off the sand and swung his AK-47 into a comfortable position. The four of them approached the prostrate group in staggered formation from the southeast over a small hillock.

The Delta operators interspersed themselves among the other trainers and knelt, blending in perfectly. Of necessity, they all spoke enough Arabic to pass if questioned.

Michael didn't check the others as it might draw attention. If they hadn't made it cleanly into place, an alarm would have been raised and the plan would have changed, drastically. All was quiet, so he listened to the *muezzin's* words and allowed himself to settle into the peace of the prayer.

Bismi-llāhi r-rahmāni r-rahīm...

In the name of Allah, the most compassionate, the most merciful...

He sank into the rhythm and meaning of it—not as these terrorists twisted it in the name of murder and warfare—but as it actually stated. It was moments like this one that drove home the irony of his long career to become the most senior field operative in Delta; his finding an inner quiet the moment before dealing death.

Perhaps it was the same experience for them in their religious fervor. But what they lacked was flexibility. They wound themselves up to throw away their lives if necessary to complete their pre-programmed actions exactly as planned.

For Michael, it was an essential centering in self that allowed perfect adaptability when situations went kinetic—Delta's word for the shit unexpectedly hitting the fan.

That was Delta's absolute specialty.

From a place of zero preconceptions, in either energy or strategy, it allowed for the perfect action that fit each moment in a rapidly-changing scenario. Among the team they'd joke sometimes about how Zen, if not so Buddhist, the moment before battle was.

And, as always, he accepted the irony of that with no more than a brief smile at life's whimsy.

Dealing death was one significant part of what The Unit did.

U.S. SFOD-D, Special Forces Operational Detachment-Delta, went where no other fighting force could go and did what no one else could do.

Today, it was a Yemeni Terrorist Training Camp.

Tomorrow would take care of itself.

They were the U.S. Army's Tier One asset and no one, except their targets, would ever know they'd been here. One thing for certain, had it been The Unit unleashed on bin Laden, not a soul outside the command structure would know who'd been there. SEAL Team Six had done a top-notch job, but talking about it wasn't something a Delta operator did. But Joint Special Operations Command's leader at the time was a form STS member, so they'd gone in instead.

Three more minutes of prayer.

Then seven minutes to help move the trainees into their quarters where they would be locked in under guard for the night, as they were still the unknowns.

Or so the trainers thought.

Three more minutes to move across the compound through the abrupt fall of darkness in the equatorial desert to where the commanders would meet for their evening meal and evaluation of the trainees.

After that the night would get interesting.

Bismi-llāhi r-rahmāni r-rahīm…

In the name of Allah, the most compassionate, the most merciful…

# # #

Captain Claudia Jean Casperson of the U.S. Army's 160th Special Operations Aviation Regiment—commonly known as the Night Stalkers—finally arrived at the aircraft carrier in the Gulf of Aden after two full days in transit from Fort Campbell, Kentucky.

The Gulf of Aden ran a hundred miles wide and five hundred long between Somalia in Africa and Yemen on the southern edge of the Arabian Peninsula. The Gulf connected the Suez Canal and the Red Sea at one end to the Indian Ocean on the other, making it perhaps the single busiest and most hazardous stretch of water on the planet.

Claudia tried to straighten her spine after she climbed off the C-2 Greyhound twin-engine cargo plane. It was the workhorse of carrier onboard delivery and from the passenger's point of view also the loudest plane ever designed. If not, it certainly felt that way. Shaking her head didn't clear the buzz of the twin Allison T-56 engines from either her ears or the pounding of the two big eight-bladed propellers from her body.

A deckhand clad in green, which identified him as a helicopter specialist, met her before she was three steps off the rear ramp. He took her duffle without a word and started walking away, the Navy's way of saying, "Follow me." She resettled her rucksack across her shoulders and followed like a one-woman jet fighter taxiing along after her own personal ground guidance truck.

Rather than leading her to quarters, the deckhand took her straight to an MH-6M Little Bird helicopter perched on the edge of the carrier's vast deck. That absolutely worked for her. As soon as they had her gear stowed in the tiny back compartment, he turned to her and handed her a slip of paper.

"This is the current location, contact frequency, and today's code word for landing authorization for your ship. They need this bird returned today and you just arrived, so that works out. It's fully fueled. They're expecting you." He rattled off the tower frequency for the carrier's air traffic control tower, saluted, and left her to prep her aircraft before she could salute back.

Thanks for the warm welcome to theater of operations.

This wasn't a war zone. But it wasn't far from one either, she reminded herself. Would saying, "Hi," have killed him? That almost evoked a laugh, she hadn't exactly been chatty herself. Word count for the day so far, one, saying thanks to the C-2 crewman who'd rousted her from a bare doze just thirty seconds before landing.

The first thing she did was get into her full kit. She pulled her flightsuit on over her clothes, tucking her long blond hair down her back inside the suit. Full armor brought the suit to about thirty pounds. She shrugged on a Dragonskin vest that she'd purchased herself giving her double protection over her torso. Over that her SARVSO survival vest and finally her FN-SCAR rifle across her chest and her helmet on her head. Total gear about fifty pounds. As familiar as a second skin, she always felt a little exposed without it.

Babe in armor.

Who would have ever thought a girl from nowhere Arizona would be standing on an aircraft carrier off the Arabian Peninsula in full fighter gear.

If anyone were to ask, she'd tell them it totally rocked. Actually, she'd shrug and acknowledge that she was proud to be here… but she'd be busy thinking that it totally rocked.

The Little Bird was the smallest helicopter in any division of the U.S. military and that made most people underestimate it. She loved the Little Bird, it was a tough and sassy craft with a surprising amount of power for her small size. She also operated far more independently than any other aircraft in the inventory and, to her way of thinking, that made it near perfect.

It seated two up front and didn't have any doors, so the wide opening offered the pilot excellent field of view. The fact that it also offered the enemy a wide field of fire is why she wore the secondary Dragonskin vest. The helicopter could seat two in back, if they were desperate—the space was small enough that her ruck and duffle filled much of it. On the attack version, the rear space would be filled with cans of ammunition.

In Special Operations Forces, the action teams rode on the outside of Little Birds. This one was rigged with a bench seat along either side that could fold down to transport three combat soldiers on either side.

Claudia wanted an attack bird, not a transport, but she'd fight that fight once she reached her assigned company. For now she was simply glad to be a pilot who'd been deemed "mission ready" for the 160th SOAR.

She went through the preflight, found the bird as clean as every other Night Stalker craft, and powered up for the flight. Less than a hundred miles, she'd be there in forty minutes. Maybe then she could sleep.

# # #

As the rapid onset of full dark in the desert swept over the Yemeni desert, Michael and Bill moved up behind the main building that was used by the terrorist camp's training staff. It was a one-story, six-room structure. Concrete slab, cinder block wall, metal roof. Doors front and back. The rear one of heavy metal was locked but they had no intention of using it anyway.

The intel from the MQ-1C Gray Eagle drone that the Night Stalkers' intel staff had kept circling twenty thousand feet overhead for the last three nights had indicated that four command-level personnel met here each night. Most likely position was in the southeast corner room. Four of the other rooms were barrack spaces that wouldn't be used until after the trainers had all eaten together at the chow tent. The sixth room was the armory.

Dry bread and water had been the fare for the trainees. Over the next months they would be desensitized to physical discomfort much as a Delta operator was. Too little food, too little sleep, and too much exercise especially early on to weed out the weak or uncommitted.

He and Bill squatted beneath the southeast window which faced away from the center of the camp; only the vast dark desert lay beyond. Shifting the AK-47s over their shoulders, they unslung their preferred weapons—Heckler and Koch HK416 carbine rifles with flash suppressors that made them nearly silent.

Bill pulled out a small fiber optic camera and slipped it up over the window sill. Squatting out of sight, the small screen gave them a view of the inside of the target building for the first time.

Not four men but eight were seated on cushions around a low table bearing a large teapot. He recognized five from various briefings and three of them were Alpha Tier targets. They'd only been expecting one Alpha.

There was a long table sporting a half dozen laptops and a pair of file cabinets standing at one end. They hadn't counted on that at all. This was supposed to be a training camp, not an operations center.

They were going to need more help to take advantage of the new situation.

He got on the radio.

# # #

"U.S.S. *Peleliu*. This is Captain Casperson in Little Bird…" she didn't know the name of the bird. She read off the tail number from the small plate on the control panel. "Inbound from eighty miles at two-niner-zero."

You didn't want to sneak up on a ship of war that could shoot you down at this distance if they were in a grouchy mood.

"Roger that, Captain. Status?"

"Flying solo, full fuel."

"In your armor?"

"Roger that." Why in the world would they… Training. They'd want to make sure she wasn't ignoring her training. Kid stuff. She'd flown Cobra attack birds for the U.S. Marines for six years before her transfer and two more years training with the Night Stalkers. She wasn't an—

"This is Air Mission Commander Archie Stevens," a different voice came on the air. "Turn immediate heading three-four-zero. Altitude five-zero feet, all speed. You'll be joining a flight ten miles ahead of you for an exfil. We can't afford to slow them down until you make contact, so hustle."

She slammed over the cyclic control in her right hand to shift to the new heading.

Okay, maybe not so much a training test.

Exfil. Exfiltration. A ground team needed to be pulled out and pulled out now. She'd done it in a hundred drills, so she kept calm and hoped that her voice sounded that way. She expected that it didn't.

"Uh, Roger." Claudia had dozed fitfully for six hours in the last three days and most of that had been in a vibrator seat on the roaring C-2 Greyhound. No rest for the weary.

Once on the right heading, she dove into the night heading for fifty feet above the ocean waves and opened up the throttles to the edge of the Never Exceed speed of a hundred-and-seventy-five miles an hour.

The adrenaline had her wide awake before she reached her flight level.

Available pre-order now
and everywhere March 2015.

For more information on this and other titles,
please visit www.mlbuchman.com

CPSIA information can be obtained at www.ICGtesting.com
Printed in the USA
LVOW06s2027240215

428171LV00001B/36/P

9 780692 336687